SIMON

Servant Siblings Series: Book 6

JENIFER JENNINGS

For Charlotte, I pray God uses you for His kingdom.

"...And there arose on that day a great persecution against the church in Jerusalem, and they were all scattered throughout the regions of Judea and Samaria, except the apostles."

-Acts 8:1

CHAPTER 1

33 A.D., Jerusalem

Simon watched James leave the potter's house heading for Emmaus. His older brother had left orders to continue with repairs to their host's home while he went to invite Lazarus and his sisters to join them in a caravan back to Nazareth. The heat of political persecution and rumors about Jesus had proved too much for the newly appointed patriarch.

In the weeks since they'd come to Jerusalem, Simon had lost his oldest brother to a Roman cross and seen their family friend beaten in the streets for being wakened from the dead. Now, with authority heaved onto his shoulders, James' first orders were to flee.

The idea of running from Rome caused Simon's stomach to flop. Was everyone in his family truly as weak as everyone claimed Nazarenes to be?

Jude passed him with an arm full of supplies. "Coming?"

Simon lifted a curious brow at his brother. "Where?"

"Naomi's." Jude flicked his chin toward the neighboring house. "James said we're to make repairs to her place as well."

Simon let out a disgruntled noise. "It's not enough we've slaved on the potter's house. Now James has peddled us out as indentured servants for the midwife, too?"

"We owe a great debt." Jude adjusted the items in his hands. "Benjamin has provided for our needs well beyond what was expected of him. He's a poor potter."

Poor. The word sent heat through Simon's veins. "He, and everyone else, are made only poorer by the taxations of Rome."

"Not this again." Jude hung his head. "When are you going to release Rome from the blame for all your troubles?"

Simon's jaw clenched. He'd despised Rome and her soldiers from the time he was a young man, having witnessed their cruelty firsthand. "I will release them when they release our people from their control."

"Simon, when are you going to understand? People are the casualties of this war; they're not our enemy."

"Didn't the prophet Isaiah say, 'They will take captive those who were their captors, and rule over those who oppressed them'?"

"Isaiah also said, 'For the Lord is a God of justice; blessed are all those who wait for him.'"

"I'm tired of waiting." Simon tightened his hands into fists at his sides. "There have been too many Messiahs and all of them have come to naught. Jesus claimed to be Messiah and didn't stick around long enough to make any actual changes. In three years, all he accomplished was a lot of talk and a collection of worthless followers. Then he went and got himself killed by Rome and now lays rotting in a borrowed tomb while we're still under their hobnailed sandals."

"Rome doesn't care about us." Jude's face pinched inward. "They're blood-drenched peacocks bent on keeping peace and expanding their territory. The true persecution of our people comes from our own."

"The council?" Simon's brow lowered. "You know they're controlled by Rome, too."

Jude groaned and turned away.

"It's true." Simon stepped forward. "Every one of them has bought their way in by filling the money pouches of Roman authorities."

"We don't have time to argue about this," he called over his shoulder. "James said—"

"I don't care what James said." Feeling heat rise on the sides of his neck, Simon turned back toward the potter's house. He wasn't going to lose another verbal battle with his scroll-smart brother. "You can break your back repairing the midwife's house, but you'll do it without me." He stomped his way inside.

Chatter of women bounced around the open area of the simple home as the scent of grains and spices filled Simon's flaring nostrils. His three sisters and the potter's daughter were hard at work, but their endless jawing ground on his frayed nerves.

He'd grown sick of being ordered around by his brothers and even sicker of being confined to the potter's dwelling. If James was preparing for them to return to Nazareth, then he was going to soak in as much freedom as he could before the trip.

Climbing the ladder to the upper room, he searched through his brother's belongings. James was as predictable as the rising sun. It was easy to find his money pouch and even easier to lighten it by a few coins. A small deposit for all Simon had endured.

Setting things back to their proper order, he donned his gray cloak and left the house without a word to anyone.

Wandering the Lower City, Simon filled his lungs with fresh air. His leg muscles found new life while he explored street after street. He couldn't recall the last day he'd been allowed to order his own steps.

For hours, Simon traveled the dusty roads of Jerusalem, unsure of where to go or what to do. All he knew was that he wasn't ready to return to Nazareth. He was not yet ready to go back to the small town where everyone knew his name and his family's business. Not yet ready to tuck his tail and run away as James seemed happy to do. Not yet ready to return to the quarry with little plans for the future.

The buildings around him grew in stature. Lively sounds from an inn called to him.

He paused at its open door and bathed in the oil lamp light. It had been years since he stepped foot inside an inn. Memories of the last time sent icy waves down his back.

Sounds of merriment and the smell of a promise of a warm meal beckoned him. He knew if he returned to the potter's house there would be an equally warm meal waiting, but there would be no revelry.

Reaching inside his tunic, he produced the coins he'd taken and twisted them around in his hand. A meal without the judgmental glances of his siblings would be a welcome change, and maybe a strong drink to wash it down.

Pushing his memories back into submission, he stepped inside the large building.

Exchanging two mites to the Innkeeper, he accepted a bowl of warm stew and a cup of strong wine and found a place to sit among the collection of travelers. Pillows of all shapes and colors were strewn about the room, offering a better place than the packed earth for weary backsides. The chunky broth heated his insides while the wine soothed his tensions.

Jerusalem never lacked for variety. Simon saw people of varying lands scattered around the open space of the simple inn like stars decorating the night sky. Languages he'd never heard mixed with the ones his tongue and ears knew.

Above the hum of life, the song of a large man reached Simon. He recognized the words as a song of David. Adjusting on his cushion, he located the source. A group of three men bantered back and forth while raising cup after cup to their lips.

Simon could tell they were Jews from the blue and white tassels that hung from the hems of their garments, but they didn't act like the docile men he'd grown up around in Galilee. These men were loud, unashamed, and boisterous. He drew closer to them like a moth to a flame, edging as close as he dared.

One man raised his cup above his head and sang, "Contend, O Lord, with those who contend with me; fight against those who fight against me!" He lowered his cup and stuck it out toward the man to his left. "Take hold of shield and buckler and rise for my help! Draw the spear and javelin against my pursuers! Say to my soul, 'I am your salvation!' Let them be put to shame and dishonor who seek after my life!" He leaned on the man to his right. "Let them be turned back and disappointed who devise evil against me!"

The man pushed him off.

But the first continued undeterred, "Let them be like chaff before the wind, with the angel of the Lord driving them away! Let their way be dark and slippery, with the angel of the Lord pursuing them! For without cause they hid their net for me; without cause they dug a pit for my life. Let destruction come upon him when he does not know it! And let the net that he hid ensnare him; let him fall into it—to his destruction!"

The other two laughed, cheering on the first man's display.

Over the edge of his cup, the man who shouted David's song peered at Simon. "Problem?"

Simon glanced over his shoulder.

"Yeah, you."

Simon shook his head. "I was simply listening to your melody."

The man next to the singer elbowed him. "And a lovely voice you have, Dan."

"Stuff it, Levi." Dan shoved him with his elbow.

Simon lifted his cup to his lips and took a small sip. The wine was doing much to steady his courage. "I was curious as to the reason for your celebration."

"Reason?" Dan leaned closer to him. "Why, we're reveling in the downfall of our enemy." He raised his cup and chugged the rest of its contents.

Levi and the other man cheered.

Simon twisted the empty cup in his hand, wishing it would refill itself. "Who's your enemy?"

Dan squared his intense gaze. "Rome."

Simon fought the twitch at the corner of his mouth before it turned into a grin. He couldn't believe his fortune to find men who seem to share his opinion on Rome. "And who has declared Rome your enemy?"

"Torah!" Dan slammed his stone cup to the ground.

"Torah!" Levi and the other man repeated.

"It is Torah that teaches us three things." Dan counted each out on his fingers. "Adonai is the only king we should acknowledge. We should establish His reign by rooting out any form of paganism and throwing off the yoke of our tyrants. And, finally, Adonai has made us separate from the Gentiles. Which means, as Adonai's chosen people, we're promised victory over our foes."

"Victory!" his two companions shouted in unison.

Dan pointed his finger in Simon's face. "That means our sovereignty is a divine right given to us by Adonai. No foreign power has any right to rule us." He shook his finger and waved it away. "And anyone who compromises or forms an alliance with Rome is equally guilty and should be treated with no less restraint." He lifted his hand toward the ceiling. "Adonai is our only Ruler and Lord."

Simon allowed his lips to slide into slight smile. "I'm in agreement with you."

"So says your words." Dan sneered and leaned back. "What have your actions to say about it?"

Simon let his gaze drop.

"Thought so." Dan squinted at him. "What's your name?"

"Simon ben Joseph."

Dan's left eyebrow rose. "And your trade?"

"Masonry mostly." Simon lifted his shoulders. "Though I've been trained to work with wood and other materials as well."

Dan rose from his pillow and circled behind Simon. He gripped the back of Simon's arm. "Strong. I'll give you that. But your strength might be wasted on stone."

Simon lifted his gaze to stare at Dan. "I assure you; it has been."

Dan chuckled. "Some fire. I like that." He rubbed his bearded chin. "How would you like to wager your zeal?"

Simon rose to his feet. "How?"

"First your zeal must be tested." Dan gripped his shoulder. "We'll see if your fire burns as hot as you claim."

"I'm willing to do anything to prove myself."

CHAPTER 2

Simon stared at Dan, waiting with held breath for the man to acknowledge his vow.

Dan kept his focused gaze for a long moment. "If your word is true, then follow us." He motioned to the others with a tilt of his head and moved toward the door.

"Now?" Simon's chest tensed as the men passed him.

Dan turned. "Do you need someone's permission?"

The verbal blow hit its mark in Simon's cracked resolve. He lifted his chin. "Lead on."

Simon followed the three men out of the inn, through the twisted streets of Jerusalem, and into the heart of the Lower City. Evening had come and gone while inside the inn and the night's shadows now blanketed the city.

Working his inner cheek, Simon glanced in the direction of the potter's house. His family and their hosts would have completed their meal and began preparations for sleep. Would they have noticed his absence among them?

Dan hesitated and put a hand on Simon's chest, halting his steps. "Better wait here." He flicked his chin. "Come on, Levi."

Obeying, Simon stood still in the nearly empty street. A few men tucked into a nearby building and a small group of others walked around a corner. Simon turned toward the man Dan had left with him. "I didn't catch your name."

The third man swayed like a head of wheat on a windy day. "S-Seth."

Simon looked around. By his estimation, they were near the Pool of Siloam. "Where are we going?"

Seth put a finger to his lips. "S-s-sh. They don't like questions."

The man's breath was heavy with wine and his extra syllables testified he may have had more than his system could handle. Simon flicked his gaze upward. Drunkenness was not a condition he tolerated. If a man couldn't hold his drink, he shouldn't hold his cup.

It wasn't long before Dan and Levi returned.

"Come on." Dan waved to Simon. "This way."

Following, Simon went down a narrow alley, around a corner, and across a street before stopping at the doorway of a house.

Dan, Levi, and Seth continued inside without hesitation.

Simon paused. He looked to his right, staring down the street. Shifting, he turned to gaze to his left. The streets were empty, not unusual, but something about the house seemed imposing, almost threatening. It was as if the house, or what was inside, shouted a warning to stay away.

His eyes traveled to the doorpost in front of him. Whatever waited on the other side would challenge his life's path. He could feel it in his bones. Though he wasn't sure what it was, he was sure it was more than his family or Nazareth could offer. With a deep breath, he ducked inside.

It took a moment for his eyes to adjust to the lamp-lit room. Several large men filled the area, all set dark eyes on him. One of the larger men stood at the end of the room.

"Come forward."

The deep voice sent a shiver through Simon, but he obeyed. Edging closer, he looked on one of the most famous faces in Jerusalem. Barabbas. He'd only ever heard whispers of the name and seen snatches of the man. Yet, here he stood in a towering presence over the group. His dark beard and wild hair doing a poor attempt at hiding several scars that marred his face. Simon found himself face to face with the most famous Zealot in Jerusalem.

Dan stood near Barabbas. "May I present Simon."

Simon inclined his head toward Barabbas. "An honor."

Barabbas' eyes traveled up and down Simon. "You bring me a mangy pup when I've asked for soldiers?"

Simon saw a large vein on the side of Barabbas' neck pulse. He knew the question was not directed at him.

"True, he's no soldier." Dan lowered to one knee. "But he's strong, a mason in fact, and he speaks with zeal."

"Speeches don't win wars." Barabbas gave a long sniff in Dan's direction. "I fear your indulgence has cost your perception." He clicked his tongue before setting his gaze back on Simon. He squinted. "You look familiar, pup. Do you dwell in Jerusalem?"

"No." Simon swallowed hard under the man's intense watch. "My fam…" He faltered. There was no reason for Barabbas to know about his family. He cleared his throat. "That is to say, I'm from Galilee."

"Galilee, eh?" Barabbas scratched at his bearded chin. "Where about?"

Simon hesitated to answer. He knew his village's poor reputation and how well known the fact was to everyone else. "Nazareth."

"Nazareth?" Barabbas' eyes widened. "Any relation to the one they call Jesus from Nazareth?"

Simon flinched at his brother's name. When he saw Barabbas' head tilt forward, he knew he'd revealed his answer without opening his mouth. There was no reason to deny it. "He was my brother."

"Was?"

"He died a criminal's death."

"Oh, I'm well acquainted with his death." Barabbas paced the small area in front of Simon. "In fact, I owe my freedom to him."

Simon lifted a brow. "Pardon?"

Barabbas paused, but kept his back to Simon. "You know the tradition of releasing a prisoner on Passover?"

"Of course."

Barabbas turned and spread his arms out.

Simon's stomach clenched. "You?"

"In exchange for your brother." Barabbas pulled his arms up into a shrug. "Though I'm sure it was all a ruse by Pilate to get your brother released. The crowd must have truly hated him to release a murderer instead." He let out a deep laugh. "He was a coward anyway. I heard he only lasted six hours on his cross."

Some of the men sneered.

Simon's heart picked up its pace, but he shook away the conflicting emotions. "Doesn't matter. Jesus is dead and buried."

"Well, there have been rumors to the contrary." Barabbas folded his arms, causing his muscles to flex. "Still, they're only rumors." He moved to Dan and signaled him to rise. "Let's test our young pup."

Dan lifted himself from his position and backed away.

"Tell me," Barabbas turned his attention back on Simon, "what do you know of the martyrdom of the Seven Sons?"

Simon's mind filled with James' voice. His brother had been the first to recount to him the bloody portion of their people's history. Simon knew James had done so as a warning in an attempt to sway Simon's short temper. A lesson that had not had the effect James desired.

The story came flooding back. "Seven Jewish brothers were seized, along with their mother, by the Syrian ruler, Antiochus IV. They were commanded to prove their obedience to him by eating the flesh of pigs. They refused."

Barabbas waved him on. "Continue."

More details of the tale came to Simon's mind. "One by one, the oldest six sons were executed, but not before enduring horrible torture. When there was only the seventh son remaining, Antiochus IV petitioned the mother to convince her last son to comply so that he might live. Instead, she urged her son to follow in the path of his brothers. In doing so, the remaining son was killed, and the mother died as well."

"Sounds like the pup knows his stuff." Barabbas chuckled and some of the others joined in. "But what does this teach us?"

Simon measured the story and the lessons James attempted to convey. His brother had told him the seven sons and their mother died horrific, painful deaths. Simon had always admired their faith in the face of foreign oppression. "I suppose it best totaled in the words of the fourth son, 'It is my choice to die at the hands of mortals with the hope that Adonai will restore me to life.'"

Barabbas' smile twisted upward.

Bolstered by the look of satisfaction, Simon added, "They were willing to die for the sins of our nation. No matter what Antiochus IV did to them, Adonai would bring them into His presence and resurrect their bodies."

"Well said." Barabbas nodded. "Tell me, do you know what our goal is?"

Simon looked around the room of men before returning his attention to Barabbas. While he'd been warned of the dangerous actions of the groups who believed violence was an effective tool to gain victory, he knew little more about them. He shrugged.

"To remove the yoke of the gentiles from our shoulders. A burden we have been carrying for far too long." Barabbas tugged at his beard, twisting the end around his finger. "How well do you know the origins of our zeal against Rome?"

Working the inside of his cheek, he glanced at Dan.

"Barabbas speaks of Mattathias."

More lessons returned to Simon's thoughts. "Mattathias was the Jewish priest who revolted against Antiochus IV and took his five sons into the hills to wage war against the Syrians."

Barabbas nodded. "Do you recall the name of the only son who survived to see his father's zeal succeed?"

"Simon." The name was heavy on Simon's lips.

"It seems Adonai has brought us a Simon." Barabbas stepped closer to Simon. "We shall see if you live up to your namesake." He turned away. "Oh, and speaking of names…" he turned back. "…I was called Jesus by my mother before taking on the name Barabbas. Guess your brother and I have a few things in common."

The weight of Barabbas' words hung on Simon like a wet cloak, but the eagerness to prove himself boiled in his soul.

For the next five days, Simon stayed in the house with the other men. He sat at Barabbas' feet listening to more stories of the Zealots and their shared yearning to remove Rome from power over their people.

He answered question after question, revealing his ability to soak in the lessons. Each hour spent with the group strengthened his soul more than the hours in the quarry had done for his body or the years spent with his family had done for his mind. Among these men he felt not only a sense of belonging he'd never known, but a bond of like-mindedness and common desires he'd not found in Nazareth or anywhere else.

After a morning of lessons, Barabbas spoke to him privately. "I think it's time for a test."

"I'm ready."

"We shall see." He rose from his place and called Dan and a few others closer. "We're taking the pup with us today."

Dan shot Simon a glance. "You think he's ready?"

Barabbas took a moment to look Simon up and down. "That's what today will tell me." He set firm eyes on Dan. "Keep him close."

Without question, Simon followed the men out of the house and toward the market street.

Barabbas and the others spread through the busy area.

Simon stayed beside Dan. "What are we doing?"

"Shh." Dan brushed his fingers over a display of jewelry. "Close your mouth and open your eyes."

Simon kept his gaze shifting from Barabbas to the booths and back again.

People ebbed and flowed around them.

Among the crowd, Simon's heart beat faster and his hands dampened. No one had told him why they were in the market or what Barabbas had planned, but Simon could feel the pulse of excitement coursing through his body.

With a simple nod from Barabbas, the group moved across the street and gathered together.

Simon had some trouble keeping up. It seemed the others spoke a silent language he had not yet learned.

In a flash, the four of them surrounded another man and, before Simon could blink, Barabbas pulled out a dagger and stabbed the unsuspecting man.

The stranger collapsed to the ground.

Barabbas and his followers turned away and spread through the street again.

Simon hurried after them, keeping as close to Dan as he dared. Pressing into an alley, he heard a woman's scream echo down the street. His steps quickened, attempting to keep up with the others. Rushing through the streets, Simon's skin burned with a heat he could not name.

They reached the building where Simon first met Barabbas and they all tucked inside.

Catching his breath, he turned to Dan. "Who was that?"

"A Roman Senator." Dan spat.

"Why did Barabbas stab him?"

"Because he was an important Roman and now... he's a dead Roman." Dan laughed. "The best kind."

Simon's stomach turned, but at the same time, he felt a strange sense of accomplishment.

"Simon," Barabbas' voice boomed through the room.

In the last five days, Simon had learned much. The chief lesson was to come when Barabbas called. He hurried across the room and stopped in front of his leader.

"You kept up." Barabbas smiled, accentuating the scars on his face.

Simon swallowed hard.

"I want to make it clear that victories in war are never achieved through words." Barabbas lifted his dagger to Simon's cheek. "Victories are secured by the point of a sword and the might of soldiers."

Simon feared nodding in agreement with the cold metal pressed against his face.

"Now." Barabbas returned the weapon to his belt. "I say you've earned this." He motioned for Levi to come forward.

Levi held out a wrapped item to Simon.

With care, Simon lifted the bundle and unwrapped it. A beautifully crafted sica lay in his hands. Gripping the handle, he held up the dagger, allowing the slightly curved blade to catch the light of the oil lamps. The rush that came with the weapon was unlike any he'd felt in his life.

"May your blade taste the blood of a thousand Romans."

Barabbas' words sounded like a prayer and a challenge tied into one. Simon liked the sound of it.

CHAPTER 3

The following morning, with his dagger secured to his side and his leader's growing trust, Simon was elected to make the day's purchases from the market.

It was a responsibility he accepted with pride. Though, part of him considered the only reason he was selected was because the others didn't want to show their faces in the market so soon after the attack on the Senator.

Simon traversed the narrow, winding streets recounting the list of items he was to secure. The market hummed with life as he passed vendors hawking their wares, their voices merging into a tumult of sound. Scents of spices and freshly baked bread wafted through the air, mingling with the dust and sweat of countless travelers.

It was weeks after Passover, but many Jews would remain in the city with the next pilgrimage feast so close. Though several of the Roman authorities would soon take flight to their far-off palaces. Simon hoped Barabbas' message delivered by dagger would encourage more of the rats to abandon the city.

Rummaging booth by booth, Simon's thoughts went unbidden to his family. It had been days since he last saw them. Surely, they had left Jerusalem with Lazarus and his sisters among the first caravan heading north that James could secure.

A twist of jealousy and animosity soured his stomach. He was glad they were gone so their reign over him would end. Though a small part of him wondered how easily they left Jerusalem without two brothers among them. Jesus' excuse was his rotting corpse occupying a stone slab. Simon's excuse was his need to be free of the shackles of a family full of cowards. With Barabbas' group, he had discovered a new kind of family. One he felt proud to be counted among.

Simon passed the potter's booth, keeping his eyes ahead. The man had opened his home to the large family in their time of need, but Simon felt he'd been handsomely paid in coins and the sweat of his siblings' brows. He didn't owe the man even a casual glance. The old man was a fool in his estimation, and he had no desire to waste time exchanging unnecessary pleasantries.

Making careful selections, Simon soaked in the bright day, but knew he needed to return soon so as not to give Barabbas any reason to doubt his loyalty. Completing his last exchange, he headed to the end of the market street.

He turned a corner in the direction of the meeting house, but spotted a familiar face. Though partially blocked by a tan headcloth, the appearance of one of his childhood friends was hard to miss.

Martha. He almost called her name aloud, but stopped himself. What was she still doing in Jerusalem? Surely Lazarus hadn't denied James' offer to get him out of harms reach. And the protective younger brother wouldn't have left the region without his two older sisters.

He faced south, knowing his best option was to return to the meeting house and forget he ever saw Martha. She and her siblings were not his responsibility. He'd found a new path, so what concern was it of his if she was still in the city?

His gaze slipped back to Martha. What if his family stayed because they were looking for him? A moment of longing was quickly snuffed out by irritation. He wasn't going to let his family stand in the way of his new purpose.

Keeping to the shadows and giving ample space, he secured the bag that held his purchases to his belt and followed Martha through the crowded streets. He would uncover the truth of what happened since he left.

The crook of Martha's arm held a basket filled with market goods and her gaze was set toward the east. Her steps were determined as she weaved her way through the multitude as easily as a shuttle through threads on a loom.

Simon kept her pace and out of her sight until they cleared the Lower City. Memories of all the years his family visited Lazarus and his sisters crashed around him. The three siblings had become like extended family. Simon's mother often referred to the three as her Bethany children. They had endured hardships that should have turned them bitter. Instead, the small family grew closer to each other and to Adonai.

As a boy, Simon admired the two sisters and their care for their often-sickly younger brother. He'd always hoped their tenderness would rub off on his sisters, with no such fortune. His three sisters had never been cruel to him, but they'd spent many days largely ignoring the youngest brother.

When his family received news of Lazarus' death, it was a shock and great pain to Simon. It was made all the more difficult when he discovered Mary and Martha had called for Jesus to heal their brother and he had denied them. The rumors of Lazarus' return from death reached all the way to Nazareth, but Simon couldn't believe. It wasn't until his family arrived in Jerusalem for the Passover and he saw Lazarus with his own eyes that he fully believed a bodily resurrection was possible.

But what did such a miracle gain the poor man? A beating that nearly sent him back to Sheol. Simon's blood ran hot recalling the bruised and broken body of his friend. James' decision to hide him away and then run at the first chance they got had been some of the weight that had finally broken Simon's trust in his new patriarch.

Approaching the Foundation Gate, Simon realized Martha wasn't going to a house in the city, but was heading back to Bethany. If he was going to find out why she was still in the area and not with his family, he needed to reach her before she passed through the gate.

Seizing his chance in the crowd near the gate, he sprang on her and pulled her into the shadow of a building. Her muffled screams were hot against his hand. She dropped her basket as she dug into his flesh. With his free hand, he tore off the hood of his cloak, revealing his face.

She murmured his name as her eyes grew large.

"If I let you go," he whispered, "you've got to keep quiet."

She nodded against his hold.

Simon eased his fingers one at a time from her mouth, hoping that was the only force he'd have to use on her.

"Are you mad?" Martha pushed him away and her hands went straight to her hips. "Giving me such a fright like that."

It was difficult to keep his composure in the face of her typical stance, but he tried.

"You should be ashamed of yourself, Simon ben Joseph." She clicked her tongue in a fury. "I'm all for jesting." She searched the ground for her items and hurried to return them to their place in her basket. "But sometimes you boys take things too far."

Simon pressed his lips into a flat line. He didn't have time for her criticism. "What are you still doing in Jerusalem?"

"What does it look like?" She waved to the items left on the ground.

He clenched his jaw, reminding himself not to speak the harsh words clawing their way up his throat. Martha was a woman open to speaking her mind, even if her words came out sharper than she intended. "I thought you'd be halfway to Nazareth by now with James and the others."

Martha's hand hovered over an onion. "Nazareth." She snatched the root and tossed it into her basket. "Your family didn't go to Nazareth. They're still here in Jerusalem."

"What?"

She rose to her feet and wiped dust from her tunic. "They decided to stay."

Simon rubbed the side of his head. "Why?"

"Jesus."

The word sprung from her lips as if it were the only explanation needed. Simon shook his head. "Why would my family stay here simply because it's the place where our brother's body lay?"

The ends of Martha's mouth came up in a sly smile. "You haven't heard the good news."

"What news?"

"Jesus is risen."

Why did that rumor still have wings? "That's impossible."

She chuckled, picked up her basket and returned it to the bend in her arm. "Impossible as it may be, it's true."

For a single moment, something inside Simon lifted. Dare he hope for his brother's return and do as he promised? "How do you know?"

"Mary and the other women saw him three days after his death."

Simon scoffed; the flicker of hope died out like the last ember of a fire.

"After that, several of the other followers saw him."

"The testimony of fishermen is about as good as shepherds."

She stepped closer, leveling a challenging stare. "I saw him."

He crossed his arms, flexing his muscles. "The testimony of a woman is even less valuable than that of a shepherd."

"This isn't a trial, Simon. It's real life." She put her hand to her chest. "If you won't take my word for it, ask any one of the five hundred others who were with me in the valley. We saw and heard Jesus speak. He is alive. There's no question in my mind."

"And my family believed you?"

"James saw Jesus too."

His brother's name sent fire coursing through his veins. James would probably say anything to get the family to bend to his wishes. Wasn't it James who wanted them all to flee to Nazareth. Why would he make up a story about seeing their dead brother to keep them in the city?

"The two of them had their own private conversation on the Mount of Olives." Martha flicked her chin to the hill barely stretching to reach its mountain status.

"So where is he? Where's my brother?"

Martha flinched. "I don't know."

There it was. She had to be lying. "You don't know because he's lying in a cave, secure behind a stone and a Roman seal."

She shook her head. "I know this is hard to believe but—"

"It's impossible to believe." Simon's chest heaved. He was through with her attempts to twist his mind and raises his hope.

"What about my brother?"

His mind raced for an explanation he didn't have. No one had an answer for Lazarus' resurrection.

"You've seen Lazarus with your own eyes, do you deny his return?"

"Well, no," Simon rubbed at the sweat beading on the back of his neck. "But Lazarus claims it was my brother who raised him."

"And?"

"How would Jesus be able to raise himself if he's the one whose dead?"

Martha adjusted her basket to her other arm. "I don't have an answer for you, Simon. All I know is that your brother is unlike anyone I've ever known. I've known your family for years. I'd know Jesus anywhere." She lifted her dark eyes to meet his. "It was him."

Simon saw a strange light flicker in her eyes.

"To be honest, it doesn't surprise me that Jesus wouldn't stay dead like a normal person." She smiled. "He doesn't do anything like a normal person."

Doubt clung to Simon's soul. "I think you all want it to be true so much that you'd do or say anything to make it so." His shoulders fell. "But it can't be. My brother's dead and buried and all of his Messiah claims are buried with him."

"Come with me. Back to your family and the followers. Perhaps they can convince you." Martha reached out for him.

Simon moved out of her grasp. This was her aim; to return him to the yoke of his family. "I'm not going back." He stepped back, allowing the shadows to engulf him. "I'm never going back."

CHAPTER 4

Simon hurried to the meeting house with the bag of provisions bouncing at his side. It was foolish to think his family had stayed behind because they were looking for him. Instead, they held to the ridiculous hope that Jesus had risen from the dead and was walking around Jerusalem. James put all his plans on hold for a dead brother while Simon's departure had meant nothing to them. How could he be so foolish?

He entered the house only to find it empty.

Dan came from a back room. "There you are."

"Where is everyone?"

"Come on." Dan moved toward the door. "Barabbas had me stay behind to take you." He dipped through the doorway.

Simon rushed to untie the bag from his belt and deposit it inside. Exiting the house, he pulled the wooden door shut and scurried across the street to catch Dan.

"Keep up." Dan kept his gaze forward. "You're fortunate I waited for you."

"Where are we going?"

Dan paused against a wall. "When are you going to learn to follow without asking so many questions?"

Simon paused in his shadow. "When are you going to learn I always have questions?"

"Barabbas doesn't like questions and neither do I. Follow or leave." Dan pressed off the wall and continued ahead.

Simon huffed as he trailed him.

Dan tucked into a thin alley.

Cautious, Simon turned sideways to fit into the cramped space. About halfway, he stopped. Dan had disappeared. "Dan?"

"Down here."

Simon dropped his gaze to a small opening.

A flash of eyes appeared in the darkness. "Get down here. The others are waiting for us."

Easing into the mouth that was barely big enough for his large frame, Simon lowered himself. He attempted to find sure footing but discovered nothing under his feet. Losing his grip, he dropped and landed in a shallow puddle.

The smell of rot and filth penetrated his nostrils. His stomach turned, causing him to gag.

"You'll get used to it." Dan held out his arm.

Simon wrapped his hand around Dan's forearm and used the leverage to pull himself to his feet.

"Try breathing through your teeth." Dan's words sounded as if he were following his own advice. "It helps."

Simon parted his lips and sucked air through gritted teeth. The foul odors translated into sour tastes, but they were a little easier to stomach.

"Come on." Dan led the way.

Breathing through his partly closed mouth, Simon trudged through the muck. Dirty water splashed up his leg as he marched.

A crashing echo froze Simon's steps. "What was that?"

Dan hesitated for only a moment. "Probably rats."

"Rats?"

"This is their home." Dan shrugged as he continued his forward movement. "We only borrow it."

Simon searched for the creatures, his eyes adjusting to the darkness. Several quick movements caught his attention. "Do they bite?"

"Oh, yeah." Dan chuckled. "Nasty things, but they can be useful."

A tremor crawled up Simon's back as he pushed away the meaning behind Dan's comment. He'd heard stories of one of the Romans favorite dishes, stuffed rodent, but never knew a Jew to feast on the vermin.

They slunk through the tunnels until light shone ahead.

Simon pressed toward it until the light engulfed him. The sands of Judea stretched out before him like an unforgiving expanse.

He turned to see the place of the skull looming over him. A shiver ran through him at the sight of three empty wooden posts. He knew they wouldn't remain unoccupied for long. Rome's chief way of keeping their subjects in line was to make a grand display of those who stepped out of line. Any criminal whose sentence was death would find themselves tied to a beam and nailed to one of those posts. He wondered which one had held his brother.

Turning away from the mount, he hurried to draw near to Dan. "Where are the others?"

"I thought they'd be in the tunnels, but they must have grown tired of waiting."

Simon followed Dan around the city walls and toward the mount of Olives. They passed through a lush garden of well-tended olive trees and various vegetation. Scents of pungent herbs mixed with the overly sweet smell of flowers and the dry earthy aroma of olive bark.

On the other side of the mount, Simon knew the village of Bethany was close. For a moment it seemed Dan was heading that direction, but he pressed on toward the edge of the wilderness.

Among the rugged terrain, Simon trekked behind Dan until they reached a secluded camp hidden among rocky cliffs and gnarled olive trees. Unlike the cultivated ones in the garden that took on shape under the hands of the gardener, these wild trees grew of their own accord, bending and twisting in whatever direction they desired.

In the open space, Simon saw the others in the middle of training. The clang of swords and shouts from the men echoed through the air. Barabbas stood over the group with folded arms; his eyes on every movement. When someone lost their match, he shouted, "Again!"

Dan led Simon toward their leader.

"Simon." Barabbas' voice was as rugged and dry as the surrounding wilderness. "Ready to learn?"

Simon nodded.

"Good. Good." Barabbas returned his attention to the group. "Dan, take him out."

Dan guided Simon to an open area. "I'll take it easy on you the first few rounds." He put up his fists. "But no more after that."

"You don't have to take it easy on me." Simon raised his fists to his face. "I grew up with four older brothers. I know how to handle myself."

For several hours, Simon endured match after match of strength and skill that tested the limits of his endurance. When he was not fighting, he watched the others, committing every move and countermove to memory.

Under the scorching sun, Simon fought hand to hand with Dan and the others to the shouts of Barabbas ordering, "Again!"

During one match, Dan got in a cheap shot, landing squarely on Simon's jaw, knocking him to one knee.

Simon lunged at Dan but missed.

Barabbas came close. "You let your temper cloud your vision and your judgment."

It wasn't the first time someone had accused Simon of such. He adjusted his jaw.

"None of us can afford to be reckless. We must be cunning, shrewd, precise." Barabbas lifted a fist toward Simon. "Again!"

Simon spent days sparring in the wilderness. With each blow exchanged, each block countered, he felt himself growing stronger and more confident in his abilities. His muscles, which had grown firm under the weight of stone work, took on a new shape under the guidance of his warrior companions. He learned to maneuver with agility, to anticipate his opponent's every move, and to strike with deadly precision.

One afternoon, he partnered with Seth. The descending sun beat down upon them, casting long shadows across the sands as they sparred.

Simon's fists clenched as they locked eyes with fierce intensity. With a nod of mutual understanding, he lunged forward, his movements fluid and precise as they exchanged blows. Simon's muscles tensed with each strike; his senses heightened as he prepared for Seth's next attack.

Seth moved with a deceptive grace, his movements were calculated and careful as he danced around Simon.

But Simon was growing to be a formidable opponent. His reflexes were sharp and his resolve unyielding as he met Seth's blows with equal ferocity. He studied his opponent, seeking an opening in his defenses.

Simon's fists collided with Seth's flesh, producing a resounding impact.

Shaking out the impact, Seth didn't miss a step.

Locked in a circular dance, Simon kept his feet light. "What brought you to Barabbas?"

Seth stared at him, keeping his fists up. "You should save your attention for the fight." He gave a quick jab.

Simon dodged the blow. "Indulge me."

"The money."

Simon straightened, but kept himself protected.

"I enjoy gambling." Seth lifted one shoulder and dropped his head to the side. "Or, as my former wife used to say, 'making poor financial decisions.'" He circled backward.

Simon matched his strides. "You were married?"

Seth threw a punch that didn't land. "For a few years." He swung again but missed. "Got into debt. But I would not break my back being someone else's hired hand. So, I made a deal with some Pharisees."

"What kind of deal?"

"They were looking to discredit some teacher from Galilee." He grunted. "I knew my wife had eyes for one of our neighbors, so I offered the guy a portion of the payout if he went along with the trap. I knew he was in debt, too."

Simon's jaw went slack, but he quickly clamped it shut so it didn't become a target. "You set up your wife?"

Seth smiled. "I had plans to divorce her anyway. She was worth less to me than a lame mule. This way I got to pay my debts, and she'd be stoned for her crimes."

"So, it worked out for you?"

"Not the way I planned."

Simon ducked another of Seth's blows. "How's that?"

"The teacher didn't take the bait." Seth shook out his fists.

Simon marked his friend's tell as a sign he was fatiguing.

"Even though they caught my wife in the very act of adultery and dragged her right to the teacher's feet, he somehow convinced the crowd not to stone her."

"What happened to her?"

"I don't care to know." Seth threw a punch and missed again. "The Pharisees paid me, I paid my debt, and filed for a bill of divorce on the grounds of adultery. I put her away and didn't look back." He shook out his right hand. "Can we please get back to fighting. Barabbas will make us do extra matches if he finds us slacking."

Simon nodded and gave Seth a short jab to move the fight along. With his friend exhausting, he knew their match was almost done. Try as he could to keep his focus on his fists, the thought of Seth's wife dug at him. While divorce was a growing option among his people, Simon couldn't wrap his mind around Seth's scheme to be rid of his wife. Could a woman become that useless that it was better to put her away than keep her around?

Divorce was a word not spoken in his home. His mother and father shared many years together before his untimely death, but never once did Joseph speak of divorcing Mary. Simon didn't think the faithful man had it in him.

It was always his parents dream for their eight children to marry good spouses and live productive lives. Being a poor family, betrothal money was scarce. Adding difficulty to difficulty, their family carried a shameful reputation surrounding the events of Jesus' birth. Life parings were as sparse as coins.

Simon was glad his father wasn't around to see Jesus waste his adult years traveling around with a bunch of fishermen and a gaggle of random women. What would Abba have said about that?

Gazing to the other men surrounding him, he considered that this life would not encourage marriage. A wife would only be a liability to a zealot. He pushed away the memories of his father and his family. Pushed away the desire to share his life with a woman that would make his family proud. All those notions were as dead as his oldest brother.

When Simon mastered fighting with his hands, Barabbas and the others taught him to wield his dagger and a sword. During breaks, Barabbas taught them to navigate the treacherous landscape, where to find water in unlikely places, and how to forage for sustenance amidst the barren wilderness.

Through it all, Simon's resolve remained unshaken. With each passing day, he grew more skilled in survival, combat, and militant tactics.

As the days grew into weeks, and the weeks stretched into a month, the wilderness forged him into a weapon. In the crucible of the Judean wilderness, amidst the harsh beauty of the untamed landscape, Simon found not only a new strength, but also courage unlike any he'd known. With that courage burning bright within him, he prepared to war against the forces of tyranny and oppression, and to commit to helping carve out a future where Israel would be free of Rome.

CHAPTER 5

On the way back toward Jerusalem from the wilderness, a pebble dug into Simon's foot, causing him to hesitate. "Go on." He hopped to the side of the path and sat to untie his sandal. "I'll catch up."

Slipping off the leather, Simon inspected his aching foot. A small rock clung to his heel. He dislodged the stone and flicked it away, rubbing the indention with his thumb. It would fade in a matter of hours.

Taking a moment to inspect the rest of his foot, he found no other issues. His feet had changed with the rest of his body. Though working in a quarry had toughened his feet for years, the last few weeks of sparring and hunting in the wilderness left their marks on his body.

He lifted his hands and turned them over. From the countless hours spent training, the callouses of his masonry hands had thickened as well. Tiny cuts and partially healed openings displayed Simon's growing ability to defend himself. He was changing inside and out and he approved of the evidence of his transformation.

With confidence surging, he settled the leather bottom of his sandal back into place and started to tie the straps up his ankle.

"You there."

Simon turned in the direction of the voice up the path. Two Roman soldiers headed in his direction. He looked toward Jerusalem to discover the rest of his group beyond his sight. His stomach dropped along with his pride.

"I say, Hebrew." One of the soldiers hustled ahead of the other. "Rise."

Securing his sandal, Simon considered his choices. The dagger hidden in his tunic and the zealot fire growing in his belly both pleaded to be fed, but he was alone and outnumbered. If he tried to overpower them, he'd surely lose.

He slowly stood to his feet, glad Barabbas wasn't near to see his unfortunate compliance and equally disappointed his leader was not available to relieve these soldiers of their heads.

"What fortune." The soldier closest to him slid a large bag from his back and shoved it at Simon. "Here."

The weight caused Simon to sway as he jostled the pack. He heard a clang of metal and the rustle of other objects within.

His gaze traveled over the soldier clad in hastily assembled armor. The man's stance was slightly awkward, betraying his lack of experience. A few unruly curls peeked out beneath his helmet. His youthful face bore the faintest shadow of a beard, evidence of his recent transition from boy to manhood. He didn't appear much older than Simon.

He cut his eyes to the other man whose gear lacked the polish and refinement of a more seasoned warrior. Though both of the soldiers' breastplates held dents and scratches, indications of at least some battlefield experience. The second's frame was larger and more muscular than his companion's, hinting at a life of manual labor before enlisting. Cropped hair with streaks of gray, evidence of his advanced age, showed where his helmet ended. Though he lacked the exuberance of youth, there was a quiet confidence about him.

The older soldier glared at Simon. "Ursus, you're going to trust this Hebrew with our supplies?"

"We've traveled miles and we've got a message to deliver." Ursus set an authoritative scowl on Simon. "He won't give us any trouble, Gaius." He lifted a brow. "Right?"

Simon kept Ursus' challenging stare, gripping the man's bag as heat rose in his neck. He was no donkey, but what choice did he have? Death with a blade in his hand would be an honorable one, but not on a dusty street with no one to know of his victory. Adonai might raise his body, but He'd have to find it tossed among the refuse of Gehenna where these two would be sure to deposit it if he tried to fight them alone.

"Move," Ursus barked, taking large strides toward the city.

Simon swung the bag onto his back and hurried after them. His muscles had increased under Barabbas' training, but even they resisted the extra weight of the soldier's supply pack.

Only about a mile outside Jerusalem, Simon knew he could fulfill his legal obligation quickly and rid himself of these Romans; hopefully without Barabbas and the others seeing him.

This requirement for Jews was simply another reminder from the Romans of who ruled whom. Yet, the law was clear; a Jew could be forced to carry a Roman's items but only for one mile.

Hiking after the soldiers, Simon noticed their gladiuses. The double-edged short swords hung on the right side of their belts, swaying with the rhythm of their steps.

Simon noted the formed bone grips. Leaning on Barabbas' teachings, this detail told him these soldiers were not new recruits. He'd learned at least six months' service was required before men were able to secure such honors. Still, two soldiers acting as messengers with no visible sign of rank meant they were probably lowly munifex. New recruits to Rome's army, but with at least some experience behind them.

With slow movements as not to reveal he was gathering information, he shifted toward the left. There, he sought evidence of pugios. Between a long stride, Simon caught sight of the short daggers. They were simple and lacking decorations, giving further evidence of the low rank of the soldiers.

With his curved dagger safely concealed, it would be easy for Simon to attack these men from behind. He might be fortunate enough to disarm one of them, but with both soldiers armed with two weapons, it would be nearly impossible to disarm both of them alone.

Simon's training potentially rivaled the soldiers, but he couldn't guarantee his opponents' skill levels. All signs pointed to inexperienced warriors, but that didn't mean they were completely incompetent. He'd spent the last month training in the wilderness, but that paled in comparison to months under Roman military instructions.

In the quiet of his forced march, he contemplated ways he could lead them to Barabbas and the others. The collection of zealots would surely be enough to overthrow the two soldiers. But how to get these two men to follow him into the city?

Without warning, a voice interrupted his thoughts. *If anyone forces you to go one mile, go with him two miles.*

The voice was so familiar and loud that it faltered his steps. "Jesus?" He glanced around for his oldest brother.

No one. The three of them were alone on the road.

"Keep up, Hebrew." Gaius turned only slightly over his shoulder, but didn't slow his pace. "We're nearly there."

Stumbling forward, Simon closed the space between them, falling back into a steady pace. He adjusted the pack, shaking his head.

Yet, his brother's words persisted in his mind. *If anyone forces you to go one mile, go with him two miles.*

They were familiar. A lesson Simon heard after questioning Jesus about his late return one evening some years ago. Jesus explained a Roman requested he carry his items for one mile. That day, Jesus went two miles with the Roman before returning in the opposite direction toward home.

Their mother praised Jesus for his obedience and display of grace. Simon's stomach turned at the memory of her admiration. She hadn't seen the act for what it truly was, for what Simon saw it as, an obvious display of civil disobedience. His brother displayed his resistance to Rome by forcing the Roman to undergo an illegal act. That deed had shown Simon glimpses of Jesus' plan for removing Roman rule. But when it came time for Jesus to act, he chose a cross instead of a crown.

Nearing Jerusalem, Ursus turned and held out his hand.

Simon continued past him.

"Halt." Ursus hurried after him. "Return my things at once."

Simon's rhythmic march shifted into an all-out sprint, straight toward the Antonia Fortress. An overflowing crowd of people made it easy to blend into the tide and keep space between himself and the soldiers.

"We ordered you to cease." Gaius failed to keep up.

Simon hurried his pace, counting each step and ignoring the commands from the soldiers. His heart pounded as he kept his eyes ahead. There was a chance they would snag him before he made it, and they would make him pay for the obvious act of defiance. There was also a chance he would be able to out run and out maneuver them just enough to make it to the fortress before them. It was a chance Simon was willing to take.

After a thousand paces, he halted at the entrance to the Fortress.

Only a few paces behind him, Ursus ripped his pack from Simon's shoulder. "You insolent dog." He lifted his right hand and slapped Simon across the cheek with the back of his hand. The action was a clear display of Roman arrogance. A man only used the back of his hand on someone he deemed lower than himself.

A sting spread across Simon's right cheek. He clamped his jaw. Another distant memory of his brother came forward.

Do not resist the one who is evil. But if anyone slaps you on the right cheek, turn to him the other also.

Without hesitation, Simon lifted his chin, turning his left cheek to the Roman. "Go ahead." A guttural growl rose from inside him. "I dare you."

Ursus blinked several times before his eyelids turned to slits. "Why, you filthy..." He lifted his right hand and struck another blow.

Simon's left cheek burned hot, yet his pride swelled. If the Roman thought he'd get away with insulting him with a backhand, he failed. Forcing the soldiers to slap his cheek with an open hand put them on the same level.

When Ursus lifted his hand to strike Simon again, a voice called out, "Ursus!"

The soldier's hand stopped mid-swing as he turned toward the sound. "Captain Longinus." He clinched his fist across his chest and bowed.

Longinus' tall frame and broad shoulders commanded respect as those in front of him moved out of his way. A golden eagle insignia gleamed from his breastplate, marking his rank. As he marched, his crimson cloak billowed behind him; a clear indication of his authority and leadership. "Why are you striking this man?"

"This Hebrew defied our orders, sir." Ursus bowed again. "I was simply reminding him of his place."

Simon stared straight at the captain, unafraid of the man beyond the symbols of power.

Longinus held Simon in a long gaze. "Is this true, Hebrew?"

Simon's brow lowered. "I've carried your soldier's pack two miles."

"Two?" Longinus' eyebrows jumped toward his feathered helmet. "Ursus, you know the law."

"But, sir, I only requested he go with me one." Ursus dipped his head toward Simon. "I ordered him to cease at the gate, but he kept marching."

Simon continued to hold the captain's gaze without wavering. The flames on the sides of his face dissipated, but the one in his gut flamed hotter.

"It's true, sir." Gaius stepped near Ursus. "We gave him orders to stop, but he refused us."

Simon saw something glint in Longinus' eyes, but he couldn't tell if it was fear or hatred.

"It seems he's been taught a lesson." Longinus turned to the soldiers. "Inside. Now." He marched back toward the Fortress.

Ursus threw his pack over his shoulder and gave Simon a slitted gaze. "Watch yourself, Hebrew." He spat as he passed him.

Simon kept his eyes on Ursus' back, watching the man enter the fortress. His dagger was heavy at his side. "My blade may yet taste your blood, Roman."

CHAPTER 6

A few days later, Simon splashed among the puddles of the underground, recounting the event of the two soldiers to Dan. It should have been a story he took to Sheol but Simon wrestled with the idea of finding himself in a similar position in the future. If he found the courage to tell Barabbas, he wasn't sure if the zealot would seek revenge on the warriors or rid himself of a stumbling block in a gray cloak. Dan had proven himself unquestionably loyal to their leader while also exhibiting the ability to keep his mouth shut.

Dan stopped mid-stride. "You truly carried their pack two miles, right to the fortress?"

Simon shifted around an indistinguishable pile of slop. "I got the idea from my brother."

"The Rabbi? I thought you said he promoted peace?"

"For the most part." Simon kicked a larger pool of sludge in an attempt to frighten a collection of rats ahead. "Though there were hints in his messages about how to disobey peacefully."

Dan followed his lead. "Peaceful disobedience sounds like he wanted to fight for freedom, but was too afraid to really do something."

"A lot of people are afraid." The faces of all the weak men of Nazareth flashed in his mind. "But too many of them are unwilling to do anything to change it."

"Not us." Dan lifted his chest as they marched. "We're not afraid to show Rome they can't lord over us."

Simon continued on for a short time, marking twist and turns in his mind. "So, what was I supposed to do?"

"About the two soldiers?" Dan stepped over a broken piece of stone. "Could've at least tried to take one of them out."

The option had entered Simon's mind. His skill and strength proved to be enough to hold his own in the wilderness with men he knew wouldn't take his life. Facing two Roman soldiers alone had caused more hesitation than he wanted.

He waded through a deep collection of water. The coolness on his ankles sent a chill up his leg.

Simon recalled the armored men. If he had managed to steal the breath of one, the other would have swiftly and surely repaid the debt. One for one didn't seem a good enough count in his estimation.

Dan took a sharp left. "You know we have eyes and ears all over this city."

Simon hurried to keep up. "Information is helpful in planning targets."

Dan stopped and turned toward Simon. "We get information on all kinds of activities, not just Roman."

"What kind of activities?"

Dan's brow shifted down. "How much do you know about the people who followed your brother?"

"Very little." Simon had intentionally kept to himself among the fishermen. He didn't appreciate Jesus' choice of followers.

"Well, we are aware of at least two former zealots who count themselves among their numbers."

"Numbers?" Simon shook his head. "What are you talking about? My brother's dead. The people who followed him are scattered."

"Perhaps they were… for a time."

Simon noticed Dan's long gaze as if the man was measuring his reactions. "If you have something to say, then speak."

"Oh, I'm merely curious." He scratched at his beard. "You tell me you allowed two Romans to live when you had the chance to rid us of at least one of them. Then I hear reports of your brother's group not only reuniting, but strengthening."

"You're going to let a bunch of fishermen stir up distrust?"

"I hear it's not just fishermen who are joining this little… now, what are they calling themselves…" He tapped his cheek. "Way Followers. That was it. They say your brother claimed himself 'The Way'."

"Even if Jesus said that, he'd be a dead end. My brother's body is rotting in a tomb."

Dan smiled. "I hear those dirty fishermen stole the body so they could make claims he rose as he said he would."

Martha's insistence that she saw Jesus crashed over Simon. Had the men from Galilee stolen his brother's body and been using it to convince people of his previous declarations? "That's mad, even for them." Simon brushed Dan and the ideas away.

"Mad as they may be, the following is growing." Dan moved to continue on. "If they become a threat to our plans, we will have to do what we must."

"Of course." Simon turned in the opposite direction.

"Where you going?" Dan called over his shoulder.

"I'll take another way back." Simon turned his attention forward. "I need some air."

"Don't run into a patrol. They might want you to carry their packs." Dan's laugh echoed through the tunnel.

Simon eased out of an opening and into the darkening streets of Jerusalem.

A breeze carried the thick scent of frankincense and burning wood from the evening offerings and mingled with the faint echoes of footsteps as people retreated to their homes for the day.

Simon navigated the intricate alleys, becoming a shadow among the shadows. Venturing under the cloak of night, the city seemed to transform, shedding its bustling daytime facade for an eerie tranquility.

He passed shuttered shops as the growing stillness seemed to seep into his bones. Yet, amid the quiet, there was a sense of unease, a tension that lurked beneath the surface.

Quickening his pace, his heart pounded as he navigated the web of streets. Each corner he turned held a promise of discovery or danger. The risks of roaming alone after dark in a city teeming with unrest and uncertainty deterred many, but the allure of the shadows was irresistible to Simon.

Venturing further, Simon noticed a figure resting against a building. He pressed himself into the shadows. Inspecting the man, he knew without a doubt who it was.

Joseph. His brother's name filled his thoughts.

In the weeks since joining Barabbas, Simon had rarely thought of his family. Between training and proving himself, he hardly had a moment to dwell on them. Martha told him of James' sudden change of plans, but Simon hoped his older brother's mind would flip again.

He watched Joseph rub his feet and legs.

What's he doing out here? His hand moved toward the curved blade inside his tunic. *He's looking for me.* The thought came with such force that Simon wondered if it had come from somewhere else. *He wants to drag me back.* He cursed Martha and himself. Surely she had informed his family of their encounter.

His eyes took in Joseph's weary form. *I bet James sent him.* His brow lowered. *I won't go back.*

With swift movements, Simon cleared the space between them, pinned Joseph against the wall, and put his forearm against his brother's neck and his blade in Joseph's midsection.

Joseph let out a sound of surprise, causing Simon to apply more pressure to his neck to cut off the yelp.

Slowly, Simon raised his head to meet his brother's frightened gaze.

"Simon?" Joseph choked out.

Simon watched realization and relief collide in Joseph's eyes.

"What's happened to you?"

He twisted his arm to cover Joseph's mouth with his hand, pressing his brother's head against the stone building. "Shh," he hissed.

Joseph mumbled against his grasp.

Simon shoved him further against the side of the building, using his body to show his force. "Stay quiet." He glanced from side to side, praying they would not draw attention. The last thing he needed was a Roman patrol discovering him. He turned back, feeling his brother settle under him.

"Good." Simon eased his blade. "Now, I have a message for you. Stop looking for me."

"But I—"

"I told you to be quiet." Simon dug his fingernails into his brother's face.

Joseph raised his arm with a slow, deliberate movement and placed his hand on Simon's shoulder.

Simon shrugged off his brother's grip. He didn't know what his brother was trying to do but, whatever it was, it would not work. He slipped his hand from Joseph's mouth and pressed his forearm against his chest to pin down his arms.

"Come back. We all miss you."

"Miss me?" Simon scoffed. "How long was it before you even realized I was gone?" He drove his elbow into his brother's chest. "Everyone was so concerned about James, I bet no one even noticed that I had snuck out as soon as he left."

"I've been searching for you."

"In between joining the Way?"

Joseph flinched.

The small reaction told Simon all he needed to know. "So, it's true." He grinned. "You joined those fishermen who fawned over our lunatic of a brother." He pressed his dagger deeper into his brother, knowing he hadn't even cut through the fabric of his brother's tunic yet. "Your trust in a dead Messiah is going to get you killed."

"I would die for my beliefs as you would for yours."

Simon hesitated. He'd never heard Joseph speak in such a way before. His older brother had always been calm and even, never showing much passion for anything. He squinted. "The difference, brother, is that I would kill you for mine."

Deliberately, Simon pushed his dagger deeper, piercing through Joseph's tunic and making contact with the bare skin underneath. The combination of Joseph's heart pounding against his forearm and his blade mere moments from drawing blood sent a strange mix of sensations through Simon. His mind screamed against his actions, but the feeling of holding a man's life in his hands felt so right.

"You can't mean that."

"Don't I?" Simon pressed the blade further into his brother, proving his intent.

Joseph sucked in a breath. "Brother." The plea edged with caution. "You don't want to hurt me."

"You think I want to do any of this?" He pushed Joseph harder against the wall. "If people did what they said they would do, none of this would have to happen."

"People like Jesus?"

"Don't you say that traitor's name." Simon's blood ran hot through his veins. Hate and anger washed through him like a storm. He slid his dagger deeper. This time, it pierced Joseph's skin.

Joseph sucked in a gulp of air and turned his face to the side. "That's what all this is about?"

Simon's body shook. He could shut his brother's mouth for good with a few movements of his blade. With all his recent practice, he knew exactly where to cut. It would be quick. A sliver of mercy for his kin.

"You ran away because Jesus didn't start a war?"

Simon shook his head. "Rome started this war." He pushed his face against Joseph's. "With their invasions a-a-and their conquest. I'm simply trying to help end it."

"You can't stop Rome alone."

"Oh, I'm not alone." Simon smirked. "You think you and your assembly are the only group in Jerusalem?" He spat to the side. "We're everywhere."

"We?"

"Let's just say I found a new family. One who values my particular set of skills and passion." He increased the pressure of the blade.

"Brother, these people are not your family. Come home."

"Home?" Simon sneered. "I have no home."

"We'll go back to Nazareth."

"Nazareth?" He spat again, this time on the wall beside his brother's face. "That filthy town full of backward people and their closed minds who cower before Rome? I don't plan to put one foot in that place ever again."

"What about our sisters? Or Ima?" Joseph's voice shook. "Do you realize what your absence has done to them?"

"I am the least of their concerns. That woman you call Ima traded us for strangers, remember? And my sisters are far more concerned with marriage than they are about what's coming."

Joseph's stare intensified. "What's coming?"

"Change, dear brother. Change is coming. Not from a cross and not from talk." He gradually slid the dagger from Joseph's middle and held the bloody tip against his brother's cheek. "Change is coming. The peace we have been promised will come from the Roman blood we will use to paint these streets."

He took in one last gaze of his brother's face. "You need to find yourself on the right side of it. Or next time I will choose a less careful spot to make my point clear." He tapped Joseph's cheek with the blade and then pushed off him.

Without allowing Joseph to speak another word, Simon disappeared into the night.

He returned his blade to its hiding place, not even bothering to wipe his brother's blood from the tip. Both his blade and he had drawn blood. It was not Roman, but it would do. A cowering, compliant Jew was just as good for a first hunt. It was even more satisfying to know he had also sent a clear message to the rest of his family.

CHAPTER 7

With Shavuot only days away, Simon moved through the retreating shadows cast by stone buildings and the rising dawn. His footsteps were swift and purposeful as he followed Levi to the secluded courtyard hidden from the prying eyes of Roman patrols.

Inside, a collection of several men surrounded their courageous leader.

Simon enjoyed the space of the courtyard to the cramped meeting house. Barabbas often called them to gather here to discuss targets or practice when the wilderness would draw too much attention.

Joining the circle, Simon's pulse quickened. As much as he enjoyed physical training, these strategic sessions did much to sharpen his mental skills. He was eager to absorb every word of Barabbas' wisdom.

The leader wasted no time in launching into his lesson. "Today, we will focus on the element of surprise." His hardened gaze swept over them. "Our enemy is powerful, but they are not invincible. By striking swiftly and without warning, we can sow chaos in their ranks and weaken their grip on our land."

Simon leaned in. Strength was a powerful weapon against the trained bodies of the Roman military, but strategy could win as many battles as brute force. Maybe more.

"The Feast of Weeks is coming." Barabbas paced the area. "That means the Romans will be on their highest guard until the flow of people ebbs." He moved toward Dan. "We have word that a large caravan of supplies is headed for the Antonia Fortress."

"When?"

Simon flicked his gaze to Seth. His face revealed the same enthusiasm Simon felt in his gut.

"Soon." The corners of Barabbas' mouth lifted. "This presents an incredible opportunity to show our might and secure some provisions." His eyes shifted to Simon. "We will need everyone for this one."

Simon knew this would give him a chance to prove himself to Barabbas and the others. His eagerness bordered on hunger. Helping to bring down a supply caravan would solidify his position among the zealots.

Barabbas continued by sharing as many details as he'd received and answered concerns.

Simon committed every word to memory. His soul and his dagger thirst for Roman blood.

When there were no more words to be shared, Barabbas divided the group into pairs. The leader wasted no opportunity to hone fighting abilities.

Simon's commitment and resolve were on full display. He won every match, having taken every suggestion to heart and adjusting to each opponent as he marked their strategies and weaknesses. Fighting was growing to be as natural to him as cutting stone.

Long shadows danced across the courtyard as the sun dipped below the horizon.

Simon landed one last blow to Levi's chest, sending the man to one knee, and raising his forearm to signal his surrender.

Barabbas neared and lifted Levi by his arm to move him out of the way. "Let's see how you do with me."

Simon lifted a curious brow. "Sir?"

Setting his fists beside his face, Barabbas circled Simon.

Shaking off the surprise, Simon matched his leader's movements.

For a few long moments, Simon examined his opponent. This was the first time he'd faced Barabbas. His insides twisted with indecision. He wanted nothing more to prove himself, but his leader was famous for his temper. If Simon did too well, would he pay the price for showing off?

Barabbas' right fist came near Simon's face, but he dodged it. He threw a jab and missed his mark.

"Come now, pup." Barabbas' voice dripped. "No holding back."

Simon heard the other matches grow quiet. Without looking, he assumed the men were gathering to watch.

They exchanged blows and continued circling each other.

Simon studied every move, every step. He watched for any sign of an opening, but Barabbas displayed why he was the one in charge.

After a missed connection, Simon noticed Barabbas' right foot hesitate to step. He took the sign and threw a hard punch, hoping it would land and weaken his leader's stance.

Before making contact, Simon felt Barabba's fist against his jaw, forcing his head to twist away.

Shouts and cheers from the crowd let Simon know he was not the favored to win.

Another blow to the head doubled his vision and caused him to stumble backward. Struggling between his will to hold his own and his will to survive, Simon bent his knee to the ground and lifted his arm.

A chuckle from Barabbas and a slap to his shoulder let Simon know his leader accepted the surrender. "Not bad, pup. But you still have a lot to learn."

Simon adjusted his bottom jaw.

"Remember." Barabbas faced the group. "We fight not only for ourselves, but for future generations. Our struggle may be long and arduous, but our cause is just."

With a firm resolve and a sore jaw, Simon headed out with the group the following evening. Amidst his uncertainty of the outcome of their mission, one thing remained clear; he would not rest until his people were free from the shackles of Roman oppression. This attack would show their strength and their might in the face of their tyrants.

The sun hung low over the Judean landscape as Simon and his fellow zealots crouched in the shadows outside the city gates. His heart pounded with readiness, waiting for the first sign of the arriving caravan.

Simon glanced at his companions; each man's eyes trained on the unseen target. His gaze shifted to Barabbas, who squatted at the head of the group. Images of their fight slipped into his mind. Even though he'd lost to his leader, he'd gained new respect and admiration. He wondered if he'd get another opportunity to face him again, and if the next match would have a different outcome.

The sounds of horses and wagon wheels finally split the surrounding silence. Simon's attention moved to the distance. Dust rose from the horizon, showing a large group heading in their direction.

Simon fought the urge in his muscles to move. Any ill-timed movement would give them away. He wasn't going to be the one responsible for giving them away before their leader's timing.

As the caravan approached, Barabbas gave a silent nod, signaling the men to attack.

With practiced precision, Simon sprang into action, his movements swift and coordinated. Together with the others, they descended upon the Romans, surrounding the caravan.

Simon lit his torch in haste and raced toward one of the wagons.

Chaos erupted as the Romans scrambled to defend themselves, their shouts of alarm drowned out by the sounds of breaking crates and the crackle of flames.

Simon threw his torch onto a covered cart as a surge of excitement coursed through his veins. He watched as the fire of his torch caught and spread, engulfing the wagon in a blaze. Flames licked at the sky, casting an eerie glow over him. A warm sensation filled his insides.

With a roar of fury, Roman soldiers emerged from the smoke and flames, their swords gleaming in the firelight as they charged his direction with murderous intent clear in their eyes.

Simon withdrew his dagger and ran toward the charge. His arms and legs moved with the memory of his training. With each well-placed strike, Simon's confidence grew.

Outnumbered and outmatched, the zealots soon found themselves overwhelmed by the sheer force of the Roman onslaught.

In the chaos of battle, Simon fought with reckless abandon, his mind consumed by the urge to survive. This was not the training courtyard or the wilderness. These Romans would not surrender nor would they accept surrender. Death would be the only result of this battle.

Two Romans closed in around Simon, their swords descending like a storm of steel. With a defiant cry, he fought, his curved blade catching the firelight as he lashed out at his enemies with every bit of his strength. The shame of complying with the two on the road fanned the fire of his fury, fending off the ones surrounding him.

In the light of the fires, Simon caught sight of a familiar face.

Ursus, the Roman who'd forced his burden upon him, squinted through the haze.

Simon stood tall, his muscles tense with anticipation, his eyes locked on his adversary with a fierce determination. Overcome with purpose, he charged the young soldier.

With a guttural cry, Ursus lunged forward, his sword arcing through the air with deadly precision.

Simon met his blow, the clatter of their weapons sent waves through his arms and shoulders.

They danced in the sand, their movements a blur of speed and skill as they exchanged blows with a ferocity of desperation.

With each strike, Simon felt the weight of his oppressors' power bearing down upon him, fueling his determination to fight and stay on his feet. He ducked and weaved, his senses attuned to the rhythm of the battle, his mind sharp and focused as he sought weaknesses in his opponent's defenses.

He discovered Ursus was a skilled fighter. His movements were disciplined and precise as he pressed the attack with persistent determination.

Simon felt the sting of his opponent's blade as it grazed his side, a searing pain that only fueled his rage. He launched himself at the Roman, his sword flashing in the darkness as he unleashed a flurry of blows.

The Roman staggered backward under the onslaught, his defenses faltering under the relentless assault.

As victory seemed within Simon's reach, Ursus rallied, his sword finding its mark with a brutal efficiency that sent shockwaves of pain coursing through Simon's body.

With a cry of anguish, Simon stumbled, his strength waning as he fought to stay upright. His vision blurred and his limbs grew heavy with exhaustion. With a defiant grunt, he surged forward, his sword slicing through the air as he unleashed a final desperate assault against the warrior.

Ursus met his blow with a swift counterattack, their swords clashing with a deafening clang.

Caught in a whirlwind of violence, Simon faltered, his body wracked with pain as Ursus closed in. Staring into the eyes of his enemy, he yielded to the inevitable. If this was to be his final battle at least he would go to Sheol with a dagger in his hand and Roman blood on his tunic.

Ursus lifted his short sword.

Simon fought against the surge of pain in his arm to raise his curved blade.

With a howl of rage, Barabbas rushed into the middle of their fight, his sword clashing against the Roman's blade.

The sound of triumph rang around Simon. He found new strength with his leader at his side. Together they pushed back against the tide of Roman aggression.

Simon's reignited urge quickened his steps until he made his way between Ursus and Barabbas. Swinging his curved blade, Simon found his mark with precision.

Ursus let out a painful cry and staggered backward, holding his side.

Simon watched the wounded warrior lower one knee to the ground, defeated but not broken. The memory of each and every time he watched one of his opponents kneel before him danced in mind. Each bolstered his courage, but none as sweet in victory as this one.

"Take care of him." Barabbas fled toward the others.

Simon's chest heaved with exertion as he stepped closer to his enemy. Hovering over the soldier, he raised his dagger.

Slowly, Ursus lifted his head.

Staring into the young warrior's eyes, Simon expected to find defiance. Instead, amid the sounds of war and the smoke of battle, he discovered fear in the dark orbs of the young man. The unexcepted sight caused him to waver. His arms burned with fatigue, his body ached with exhaustion, and his mind warred with hate and hesitation.

One slice would end the man kneeled in front of him. One clean slice and another Roman would fall. His blade would drink of its enemy's liquid life and he would taste victory. He raised his dagger higher, pressing the curved blade near the soldier's throat.

Ursus closed his eyes as if to welcome the final blow.

Simon's arm locked. His muscles tensed against an unseen force. Glancing around, he saw his companions fleeing into the night. Their arms full of precious spoils and their howls full of success.

He looked down at Ursus.

The soldier's eyes remained closed, his breathing growing steady.

Lowering his weapon, Simon allowed the shadows of night to swallow him while the heralds of rebellion echoed around him.

CHAPTER 8

Simon made his way through the bustling streets as throngs of people gathered in the market. In the days leading up to Shavuot, he'd healed physically of his wounds, but he had not been able to shake the look of fear in Ursus' eyes. Something that night forced him to spare the soldier's life. He was unsure if the source was divine or his own fracturing convictions. Whatever it was, the choice plagued him.

Atop a makeshift platform in the center of the market street, Barabbas towered over the crowd. Required preparations for the feast and an open market had drawn many out of their homes. The zealot leader's looming presence commanded the attention of all who stood before him as he railed against the injustices perpetrated by their Roman oppressors.

"Brothers!" Barabbas' voice echoed off the stone walls. "For too long, the yoke of Roman rule has desecrated our land and oppressed our people. But no more!"

The crowd erupted into cheers.

Among the sea of faces, Simon found himself swept up in the fervor, his heart pounded with righteous fury.

The reminder of his purpose overshadowing his concerns.

A tumult of emotions churned within him like a stormy sea as he listened to Barabbas' speech. There was a magnetic power in Barabbas' words. The fervor in Barabbas' voice stirred something deep within him, a longing for liberation from the shackles of Roman oppression that had burdened his people for generations.

Beneath the surface of his excitement, Simon felt a gnawing uncertainty, a nagging doubt that whispered of the lurking dangers. He knew all too well the price of challenging the might of Rome and the bloodshed and suffering that awaited those who dared to defy the empire. His own brother had paid the ultimate price for his peaceful rebellion and countless others with their open acts of defiance. Yet the allure of freedom was intoxicating.

While Barabbas continued to speak of overthrowing their oppressors and reclaiming their birthright as true children of Abraham, Simon felt a surge from deep within. His fists clenched with determination.

Despite his reservations, Simon couldn't deny the appeal of Barabbas's vision. The prospect of a future where their people were no longer subjugated, where they could live in freedom and dignity, was a dream too potent to resist.

Simon stepped in front of the platform, lifting his fist into the air. "We will not be silent!" His declaration rang out with a clarity that cut through the noise of the crowd. "We will not bow to these Gentiles! We will rise and reclaim what is rightfully ours!"

The horde roared in approval; their voices raised in a chorus that echoed through the streets of Jerusalem.

Around them, the city seemed to tremble with the weight of their righteous anger. The very air quivered with the promise of rebellion.

Simon heard a commotion to the north that sounded like a mighty rushing wind. He stepped aside from the front of the crowd while Barabbas continued to weave a tapestry of hope and revolt.

In the distant Upper City, Simon saw a pillar of fire seeming to come down from the clouds. He blinked, untrusting of his own eyes. When his vision cleared, the pillar was no longer visible. He shook his head. If a building was on fire, the flames would have reached upward. Why would a flame reach down to a building in the Upper City?

As the rally around him surged under Barabbas' call to arms, thunders of chaos echoed from the north and mixed with the noise of the assembly.

Simon sensed an unease growing in the air. He searched for the lingering threat he could feel in his bones. The hairs on the back of his neck stood on end. Something was coming.

Without any more warning, a larger crowd of people poured from the north and with it several bands of Roman soldiers marched toward the market. They pushed onlookers aside, shouting orders to disperse.

Glancing over his shoulder, Simon watched Barabbas disappear into the fleeing crowd. Dan, Levi, Seth, and the others all followed their leader into the confusion.

In his attempt to do the same, Simon slammed into the metal breastplate of a soldier. Peering up, he met eyes with Ursus.

The soldier stood firm. "Arrest this one."

Two others grabbed Simon's arms before he could reach for his dagger. He struggled against them, but they held firm. Glancing around, he discovered his companions were not coming to his aid. He was alone and captured by the enemy. Swinging his head back, he met Ursus' focused glare.

"Take him away."

The two soldiers dragged Simon through the streets and into the Antonia Fortress. It's looming structure cast shadows over the Temple mount and reminded Jews that Rome watched their every move.

Simon shouted curses at the men who held him and struggled to spit in their face. He kicked and fought, trying desperately to reach his weapon. The trained warriors were undeterred by his fleeting attempts to rile them into a physical fight.

Inside the Fortress, the Romans continued forward until they reached a lower chamber. In the dank confines, the guards shackled Simon and hung him from chains. Flickering torchlight cast eerie shadows across the stone walls, illuminating the faces of his captors, their eyes gleaming with malice as they circled him like vultures.

Simon kept a silent, steady glare on Ursus. Struggling had tired him, wasting valuable resources of strength. Even weakened, Simon made sure his enemy knew he wasn't giving in to them.

A soldier stepped forward. "What do we have here?"

Simon recognized Longinus; the captain who'd ceased Ursus' assault the day he carried the soldier's pack two miles. From the indifferent look on the older soldier's face, he didn't recognize Simon.

"You think you can defy us, zealot?" Longinus sneered, his voice a venomous hiss as he loomed over Simon. "It isn't enough I have to deal with the chaos of visiting foreigners in the Upper City causing trouble. Then we discover you zealots attempting to encourage an uprising. You think you can stand against Rome?"

Simon met his gaze with a defiant scowl. He fixed his jaw in a steely resolve not to expend any more energy. He would not give these Romans the satisfaction of an answer and he would save his might for whatever they would throw at him.

Longinus chuckled darkly. His lips curled into a cruel smirk. "We'll see if we can extract some answers." He motioned to the others. "Bring the tools."

With a sinking feeling in the pit of his stomach, Simon watched as others approached. They wielded instruments of pain and suffering. No matter what they did to his body, he would not betray his companions or their cause.

The Romans wasted no time in setting to work. Blows rained down upon Simon's body with a relentless ferocity that threatened to break his spirit. His barely healed wounds screamed with fresh agony.

Through the haze of pain and exhaustion, Simon clung to his lessons. Barabbas' words echoed in his mind, reminding him of their fight for freedom. With each blow, he drew strength from his training and the stories of the martyrs who had gone before him.

When the Romans paused their torture, a sense of awareness settled over him, a chilling certainty that his ordeal was far from over. He knew the Romans would stop at nothing to extract the information they sought and to crush the spirit of resistance that burned within him. These men were trained well in battle and even better in torture.

Hours stretched on. As the torment of his captivity wore on his body and mind, Simon felt the vines of doubt creep into his consciousness. Was he strong enough to withstand the relentless onslaught of his captors? Could he endure the pain and suffering that they inflicted upon him with such cruel freedom?

Within the darkness that threatened to consume him, a flicker of light emerged, a beacon of hope amid the despair.

In the depths of his soul, Simon heard the cry of the seven sons' mother resonate through him. *Do not be afraid of this executioner, but be worthy of your brothers and accept death.*

Simon hung limp from his chains, his form a fresco of bruises and cuts painted by the brutality of Roman fists. Even as his body shouted in agony, his spirit remained battered but unbroken.

With enduring determination, he met his tormentors with a rebellious stare, knowing with certainty that the cause he clung to was greater than any individual sacrifice.

Withdrawing, the Romans heaved from fatigue.

Longinus drew near. He grabbed Simon's hair, yanking his face upward. "Strong-willed, I'll give you that much." He released his grip, causing Simon's head to drop.

"Sir." Ursus stepped forward. "I don't think we're going to get anything out of this one."

"You're not trained to think."

Simon noticed Ursus' hand shake at his side before he pulled it behind his back.

"If we go much longer, we'll have a body to dispose of."

Wiping his bloody hands on a rag, Longinus shrugged. "And?"

"Wouldn't a message be better?"

"What?"

"He'll be a message to the others to cease these rebellions or they will be next."

"And if they don't heed the warning?"

Ursus slid his gaze toward Simon. "Then we've had practice for when we capture the rest of them."

Longinus' scowl turned upward. He flicked his chin in Simon's direction. "Release him."

The clank of chains lifted Simon's spirit. He fell forward, free of their cold grasp. Rising to his shaking feet, he gave Ursus one last glare.

He was unsure if the soldier's mercy was merely payment for Simon's failed attempt to kill him during the attack on the supply caravan or something more. All he was certain of at that moment was that he was free to walk out of the dark cell and toward the light of day. He would grasp that freedom and hold onto it.

This battle ended in defeat. Simon vowed the next time he met Ursus, the outcome would not be the same.

CHAPTER 9

Simon limped toward the direction of the meeting house. He took several alleyways and doubled back, cautious of anyone following him.

His steps were slow and labored, each movement sending waves of pain radiating through his battered form. The weight of his injuries bore down on him like a heavy cloak. Blood dripped from gashes on his forehead and face, staining his tunic crimson. The throb of his injuries matched the pounding of his heart, each beat a reminder of the price of resistance.

After confirming that the Romans had truly finished with him for the day and were not going to follow him to the others, he made his way to the house.

Reaching the doorway, he collapsed onto the hard-packed dirt of the interior.

Several men rushed toward him, their sandaled feet kicking up the surrounding dust.

"What happened to you?"

He recognized Seth's voice but struggled to answer through his dry throat. Lifting his eyes, he saw several men staring down at him.

"Move." Barabbas growled and shoved men out of his way.

Simon attempted to rise, but faltered.

Barabbas kneeled near him. "Explain yourself."

Simon winced as he recounted his torture at the hands of the Roman soldiers, the memory a bitter taste on his tongue. "They thought they could beat me into submission."

Barabbas's jaw clenched. "You didn't give them anything, did you?"

"Not a word."

"Those dogs will pay for what they've done." He rose to his full height. "Get him aid."

Simon closed his eyes, giving into the pull to rest.

When he opened them again, he was in the main area with Dan and Seth. They must have moved him, because he was no longer on the ground by the door, but propped against a far wall. The men's faces showed signs of worry.

He groaned, his injuries crying out against the movement. "How long was I out?"

"Not long." Dan held a cloth against one of the wounds on Simon's head. "Help's here."

Simon searched around them to see an older woman rifling through a large bag. She kept her eyes on her objects, but her hands held a slight tremor. Simon hoped it was fear shaking them and not her inability to heal.

"We can't let those Romans intimidate us." Dan dropped his hand. "We have to show them we're not afraid to fight back."

Seth nodded in agreement; his expression grim. "We'll stand against them, no matter what."

Simon's attention flicked between the two of them. "I'd be happy to repay their kindness just as soon as I'm patched up."

He turned his attention to the woman. She looked old enough to be a mother, but her hair held no gray streaks. Her skin was rough and worn like leather, but her form revealed she ate well. A headcloth held back a long braid and her tunic was simple, but clean. She dug through a large sack, producing bottles, cloths, and bundles of herbs Simon didn't recognize.

"Don't worry." Seth rose to his feet. "We'll compensate her well for her services."

Simon wondered where they found a healer so fast and one willing to enter a den of zealots.

"Come on, Dan." Seth motioned with his head. "Let's let the woman work."

The two men made their way to the other side of the room.

Simon was grateful for the space, but listened to their hushed tones. He assumed he was the topic of their conversation and pondered what orders Barrabas had left them in his absence.

The woman moved toward Simon. "I'm going to have to look at your wounds."

Simon glanced down. Seeing his exposed skin already blossoming with bruises, a flash of heat rose on the sides of his neck. Other than his mother and sisters, no woman had beheld his unclothed form.

"You can call me Tirzah." She held his gaze. "I've been a midwife for more seasons than you've seen. I promise, I'm only interested in tending your wounds."

Her gentle, and somewhat jovial, tone put Simon at ease. He shimmied off his torn outer tunic and removed the one closer to his body.

"There now, that's better." She proceeded to inspect his wounds.

Simon watched her weathered hands as they moved over his skin, pressing here and there.

Tirzah made sounds of concern as she worked toward his face. With a light touch, she turned his head back and forth, scrutinizing the bleeding areas.

Her lips pressed into a thin line of concern. "Some of these wounds are brutal."

Simon heard apprehension in her voice.

"With proper care, you'll recover." She mixed salves and unwound thick pieces of cloth. With practiced hands, she worked to cleanse his wounds and soothe his pain.

Simon shifted his glance to Dan and Seth. "So, where'd they find you?"

Tirzah didn't remove her attention from her work. "There are many of us who despise Rome, young man." She adjusted his left arm to get a better look at his side. "Some of us simply prefer not to use our fists to get our point across." She clicked her tongue. "Some of your injuries are in different stages of healing."

"Violence is the only language some speak."

For the first time, Tirzah's hands wavered. "Vengeance has a way of consuming those who seek it." She returned her focus to her task without saying anything more.

The quiet, but determined look Tirzah held while she worked reminded Simon of his mother. His thoughts drifted to the memories of wounds from the many fights and falls his mother had tended over the years. Among her scornful reminders to use his words instead of his fists, her hands still extended care and healing.

Remembering her touch and her face, Simon's insides ached. He fought to push aside the yearning for the past. There was no going back.

After a last glance over his body, Tirzah helped Simon slip back into his tunics. "I'll leave some herbs to help with pain." She returned the tools of her trade to her bag. "If you wash them properly, you can reuse those cloths." She rose and went to speak with Seth and Dan.

When the midwife was paid and escorted out, Dan and Seth took up their place beside Simon again.

"We've got it all worked out. We're going to send a reply to those Romans they won't soon forget." Seth's voice held an eager edge as he revealed their plans.

After a few days of recovery, Simon joined his companions on their mission of revenge.

A full moon hung high, casting a silvery glow over the narrow streets of Jerusalem. The city was asleep, except for a few wandering souls and the ever-watchful eyes of Roman soldiers patrolling the darkened streets.

Simon, still aching from the beating he had endured, moved silently alongside Seth, Dan, and Levi.

Their plan was simple, but dangerous. They would ambush a patrol and send a clear message to those who'd tortured Simon. Roman soldiers were predictable, making them vulnerable to a well-timed attack. They were using Barabbas' example of an unexpected attack.

Simon hoped the men who'd laid hands on him would be on patrol, but with hundreds of Romans assigned to Jerusalem, there was no way to know.

Seth led the way, his eyes scanning the shadows for signs of their enemy.

Simon felt a mixture of anticipation and fear gnawing at his insides. His body ached, but was determined. He would show Rome, and Barabbas, that nothing was going to break him.

The men took their positions in a secluded alleyway and waited.

Simon's heart pounded as he strained to listen for the telltale clink of Roman armor and their hobnailed sandals against the paved stones and packed earth.

Moments felt like hours, but finally, a patrol came into view. Four soldiers laughed and talked as they went, arrogance evident in their casual stride as they made their way along the street.

In the dark, it was difficult for Simon to make out any distinguishing features.

When they neared, Seth gave a subtle nod, the signal to move. Like shadows, the zealots emerged from their hiding place, surrounding the unsuspecting soldiers.

Seth struck first, his dagger flashing in the moonlight as it found its mark in the neck of the nearest soldier. The man crumpled without a sound, his lifeblood pooling around him.

The other soldiers reacted swiftly, drawing their swords.

Simon lunged at the closest one, rage lending strength to his weary limbs. Their swords clashed, and for a moment, Simon struggled against the soldier's superior strength. He sidestepped a blow.

That's when the dim light highlighted the face of Ursus.

He saw the young soldier recognize him in the same instant.

The two lunged toward each other.

A few stray pulses of weariness and guilt mixed with the wrath flooding Simon's veins. He struggled against the fury of the Roman, fighting with everything to lose.

Summoning his last reserves of strength, Simon twisted his blade free and drove it into the Roman's chest.

Ursus' eyes widened in shock and pain before the light in them dimmed.

Simon withdrew his blade, letting the body fall before him. Panting, his heart pounded faster than it ever had before. He glanced around to see the other soldiers fall at the feet of the others.

The surrounding street was silent once more except for the ragged breathing of the zealots. The metallic smell of blood hung heavy in the air, mingling with the night's cool breeze.

Simon allowed his gaze to drop to Ursus. The look of shock frozen on the soldier's face would stand as a beacon to those who discovered the aftermath of their ambush. He wiped his blade on the fallen soldier's tunic before sheathing it. His body screamed in protest, but the satisfaction of avenging his torture provided more of a balm to his pain than Tirzah's mixtures.

Back in the safety of their meeting house, the exhilaration of battle faded, replaced by heavy exhaustion. Simon lay down, the events of the night repeated in his mind. The faces of the soldiers, the clash of steel, and the taste of victory.

When sleep finally claimed him, the fight continued in his dreams. Though one battle was won, the war for freedom continued.

CHAPTER 10

15th of Nisan, 35 A.D., Jerusalem, Two years later

Simon pulled his gray hood over his head as he turned onto the market street. In two years, the once overwhelming collection of booths shifted from chaos into memorized details. He knew every seller, every family, every story along the long, wide road. The hum of humanity had morphed over the months into places he could gain information. He knew which sellers were sympathetic to the cause, and whose loyalty could be purchased as easily as their wares.

He experienced every season in the bustling city from blistering heat to chilly winter rains. Passover was upon Jerusalem once again bringing with it a rise in temperatures and visiting Jews. People flocked to the market like sheep to the sheepfolds seeking fantastical items from far-off places. The throng slowed Simon's progress but also provided a better harbor in which to hide. He floated through the street, keeping his gaze smooth and easy. His target would soon arrive, and he needed to be ready.

Over the years among Barabbas' flock, he proved himself time and time again. Not only besting every other man, besides Barabbas, in fights with hands or weapons, but also in mental skill and information collection. Simon discovered his handsome features could part the lips of almost every woman on the market street, and his cunning tongue could pry open the even proudest merchant.

He hunted with his zealous companions and participated in countless acts against their oppressors. His mind and body were molded into a weapon; an axe laid at the roots of Rome.

Seth had been the one to bring the current mark to Barabbas' attention. Their leader passed the mission on to Simon. This was his opportunity to show he could not only hunt alone, but follow orders with little information. In two years, Simon's ravenous hunger for answers to his every question was replaced with trust and loyalty to his leader's word. This was his hunt and another in the seemingly endless tests of Barabbas.

The sun climbed over the city walls, causing tiny beads of sweat to form on Simon's upper lip. A heaviness crawled over him. The air was thick and pricked at the exposed skin of his neck, foretelling of coming rains. This too was part of his strategy.

For days, he'd watched the growing population in the market and he kept an eye to the skies. Today, the first day of Passover, with rain on the way, was the perfect opportunity to complete his mission.

Simon played his part well, like an actor in the Greek plays he'd heard about. He kept his steps light, examining products and keeping his head down. His glances were easy and infrequent. He didn't stay at any booth too long, but he also didn't rush. The aim was to blend in, to become one with the crowd so he could disappear as fast as he needed.

After completing two rounds along the street, doubt began to creep. Everything was perfect, waiting only for the prey to arrive.

Simon took a few steadying breaths. Like an expert hunter, he could not allow worry to cloud his vision and other senses. He reduced his steps, gazing over a stall of fresh fruit. Their mouthwatering scent caused his stomach to protest. He'd been in the market for hours and his body was reminding him of his humanity in more ways than one. Ignoring the signals, he moved on. This mission was too important to be seduced by trivial matters.

After pausing at a tentmaker's booth, Simon finally spotted his target. Barabbas had repeated the details to him so many times Simon could have painted a fresco of his prey. His movements slowed; his focus narrowed. He resisted the urge to pull his dagger, waiting for the right moment.

The mark was the center of a small group, exactly as Barabbas warned. Simon would need to be patient. He moved around them with deliberate strides, checking for weak spots. He noticed one of them always moved to his right, leaving an opening. And, just as Barabbas had told, the target often tested the gaps by falling back a little more each time the group stopped.

Simon knew he only had a few openings before the group would close ranks and leave the market. With each pass, he dared closer until he was within reach. Timing his steps perfectly, he put himself closer to the mark. Without hesitation, he pulled his dagger and inserted it cleanly into the mark's upper midsection, pointing the weapon's end up and swiftly twisting it so no sound would be uttered.

Through his blade, he felt his prey's last choking breath as red spread through the thin tunic. Daring a moment of satisfaction longer, Simon looked into his victim's eyes. He reveled as light faded from the dark orbs. The thrill of the kill coursed through his veins with warmth and satisfaction. Extracting his dagger cleanly and returning it to its sheath, he watched the body crumble to the ground.

Turning to leave, a loud crash sounded above his head, causing him to glance up. Lightning cracked through the sky. Perfectly timed. The signal of rain would scatter the crowd and give him several easy paths to flee.

His gaze fell toward the mark just as the body hit the ground. The empty space in front of him revealed the group moving toward him. Rain fell, drowning the faces of the men in a sheet of water. Simon fixed his eyes on a familiar one.

Saul of Tarsus was rushing at him like an angry ox.

As quickly as the rain began, Simon disappeared into the storm and the crowd. The last sound he heard was a loud wail mixed with another clap of thunder.

Simon hurried his pace, ducking into an alley and slipping into the tunnel system. He rushed through the shallow water, rising with the rains. A few sharp turns and a long pathway took him to an opening near the meeting house.

He shimmied out and into the street, strolling into the building and closing the door behind himself. The open area was filled with several others who raised their heads as he entered.

"Simon."

Barabbas' bellow was a command to come that Simon obeyed as fast as his heart was beating.

"Is it done?"

Simon bowed. "As you've instructed."

Barabbas put his large hands on Simon's shoulders. "Well done, pup." He turned Simon toward the group. "That's how we bring down Rome. One Roman at a time, if we have to, until they get the message."

The men shouted their agreements and support.

Simon's chest swelled with his accomplishment.

The heavy wooden door swung open, revealing Seth, drenched and dripping. He marched toward Simon. "What was that?"

Simon's gaze lifted to his leader towering over him. "You sent Seth to watch me?"

"I can do as I please, pup." Barabbas glanced to Seth. "What's the issue? Did Simon complete the mission or not?"

"Why'd you change the mark?"

Simon's empty stomach flipped at Seth's accusing glare. He recounted every moment of the fresh kill and recalled every morsel of detail Barabbas had been willing to share. They matched exactly. "What are you saying?"

"The girl wasn't the mark." Seth shook his head, adding confirmation to the words.

The blood in Simon's veins went from warm to ice. "What?"

Seth's eyes traveled up to Barabbas. "You told him the mark was the Pharisee, right?"

"Pharisee?" Simon's thoughts spun. The only Pharisee he saw in the market was… "You mean Saul?"

"Reuben paid us to kill the Pharisee." The sides of Seth's neck bloomed red, but he didn't take his eyes off Barabbas. "Why order Simon to take out the woman?"

"Because killing the Pharisee was pointless." Barabbas' mouth twisted upward, the scars on his face folded with the movement. "Why slaughter a newborn lamb when the fattened calf is prime for feasting?"

Simon put his hand to his throbbing temple and stepped out of Barabbas' hold.

Seth shook his head. "What does that mean?"

"That Pharisee is new to the council." Barabbas folded his arms over his chest. "They'll wear him down to be just like the rest of those indifferent jackals." He held up a finger. "The woman was the daughter of a senator. Her blood sends a clear message to her family and the rest of those no-good Roman aristocrats."

Seth tore at his hair. "What am I supposed to tell Reuben when he finds out you switched the marks?"

"Tell him 'You're welcome' and that he owes you double for our trouble."

Thrusting his hands in the air, Seth stormed out of the house.

Simon stared at the open doorway. "She wasn't the mark?"

"But she was a good one." Barabbas smacked him between the shoulder blades. "I knew you'd make a great addition to our group." He chuckled. "Rest up. You've got another mission."

Simon blinked rapidly. "So soon?"

Barabbas winked and left.

Tightness clamped around Simon's chest. All the merriment of his triumph crashed into doubt and concern.

Simon's thoughts raced with questions. Why would anyone want to have Saul killed? Why was Saul with a senator's daughter? The chief among them sprang upon him like a lion. Who was the next mark?

Knowing Barabbas was only going to answer his questions when and if he deemed the moment right, Simon hurried out of the house to catch Seth. Perhaps Seth would be willing to share more.

It didn't take long for Simon to track Seth. He hurried to his side.

"Leave me be, pup." Seth kept a rushed pace as if he'd missed a meeting.

Simon put out his hand to stop him. "Don't call me that."

Seth pushed past him.

Matching his speed, Simon grabbed Seth's shoulder. "Tell me what happened."

Shrugging him off, Seth continued his march. "You don't know what you've done."

Simon jogged to move in front of Seth and put both his hands up to halt him. "Then tell me."

Seth pressed against his hold. His nostrils flared. "We were paid to take out the woman's betrothed, the Pharisee."

"Do you know why?"

Seth lifted a shoulder. "Something about revenge for him killing someone else's betrothed."

"Why would Barabbas switch them?" Simon dropped his hands. "Could he have made a mistake?"

"If there's one thing I've learned in all my time as a follower of Barabbas, it's that the man doesn't make mistakes. He makes measured choices." Seth stepped around Simon. "Now I'm left to resolve this issue."

Simon let him go. The vines of worry and doubt wrapped around his thoughts. Did Barabbas have other motives for wanting the woman dead or was this simply another test of Simon's allegiance?

CHAPTER 11

Simon didn't have to wait long for his next mission. After Passover was complete, and the shocking death of the senator's daughter waned, Barabbas led Simon and a few others outside the city. There, near an enormous pile of rocks that stood in front of a collection of tombs, Barabbas revealed Simon's new assignment.

"Many Romans know this rock formation." Barabbas patted one of the larger boulders. "It's here where Simon will show us the true measure of his worth."

Simon looked at the rocks. There was nothing unique about them in his estimation. They didn't seem to belong to a particular group or even show signs of being used for religious practices. There was no inscription or even signs of human use.

"Many a man can stomach killing their enemy." Barabbas circled the pile of stone. "But a true loyalist will not hesitate to rid the world of every drop of Roman blood. Including the bodies of the innocent."

Simon stared at the rocks. "I don't understand."

Barabbas clicked his tongue and caressed the top of the largest boulder. "This is a place where the Romans dispose of their unwanted infants."

Rock children. Simon was familiar with the brutal Roman practice in stories alone. He never fully allowed himself to believe a woman, any woman, could so easily cast aside her newborn like those who obeyed the ancient order of Pharoah to throw Hebrew boys in the Nile. Those of the past, at least, were under the threat of death for their disobedience.

He couldn't reconcile a mother abandoning her helpless child to die in the elements; not even a Roman. Though his own mother had practically abandoned her other children to follow the ravings of his lunatic brother. Even Jesus' death could not sever the ties their mother had to him. Her choice to stay with Jesus' equally disillusioned followers instead of returning to her desperate offspring had driven Simon mad.

He shook his head. "Why not leave them abandoned to their fate?"

"That was good enough." Barabbas continued to pace around the simple structure. "There was no better justice than to witness Romans slowly killing themselves from the inside." He came around the formation again. "That was until another group intervened." He stopped in front of Simon. "A festering cluster calling themselves 'Way Followers' has discovered this place and has been rescuing the doomed children; electing to raise them as their own."

The others made retching sounds and voiced their displeasure.

"So." Barabbas clapped his hands. "Here is where we shall see your final measure, Simon. Each child placed upon these rocks is to die by your blade."

Simon swallowed a rising lump. Roman soldiers were easy to kill, and Roman men were simpler than their armored counterparts. The senator's daughter, though the first female life Simon had snuffed out, was a satisfying victory. Infants? Would he have the stomach to do it? How many would be enough? "For how long?"

"Until I'm satisfied that the truth has penetrated your soul."

Simon tilted his head. "What truth?"

"That there is not a single Roman who is innocent. They all need to be wiped away. Conceived or converted, Romans and their way of life need to be purged from our land."

When the group departed, Simon settled up among the tombs. For two days, he waited and watched, unsure of if or when a desperate woman would appear to unburden herself.

Suddenly, his fate shifted.

A young girl appeared alone and crept near the boulder.

She was so young Simon wondered if the wiggling babe in her arms came from her womb or a master's.

Nearing the stone, she held onto the child as best she could, staring into his face. Several moments passed as the baby cried and squirmed.

Flinching at some distant sound, the girl disposed of the baby and hurried away.

Simon tensed, ready to move, but hesitated. He was alone, but it wouldn't last. Barabbas and the others would return at any moment. They stopped by often to check on him. He needed to dispose of the mark quickly or his reluctance might drive doubts into Barabbas' mind.

Peering out from his hiding place, he watched the baby flail his arms with pitiful cries. The noise sounded similar to an injured animal. Simon would make the death quick. A small measure of mercy he would afford an innocent. He rose to approach, but wavered when another form appeared.

"A baby!"

The voice was unmistakable. A tremor went through Simon. Lydia?

"Who would leave a..." Lydia's voice trailed off. "Could this be a rock child?"

The baby continued to wiggle and scream.

"How could anyone simply abandon a child like this?"

Simon kept to the shadows as he watched his sister pull off her headcloth, pick up the child, wrap him in the cloth, and cradle him in her arms. The action quieted the boy's cries.

"Oh, my!" Lydia held the boy toward the sky. "Stephen?"

Simon squinted, attempting to discover what had startled his sister. He looked around for the man attached to the name she'd uttered, but found no one else around.

"Forgive me." Lydia pressed the child against her chest once more. "You remind me of someone."

Who is she talking about? Simon couldn't help his curiosity and moved closer.

When the boy settled again, Lydia brushed his face. "You've lost someone." She rocked him gently. "I have as well." She bounced and paced in a circle. "What am I to do with you?"

As Simon moved closer, a voice startled him.

"We'll be happy to dispose of that refuse for you."

Barabbas, along with Dan, Seth, and Levi moved in to circle his sister.

Lydia froze, cradling the boy against herself. "What do you want?"

Simon joined the others, shifting himself behind Seth's back.

Barabbas took a step toward her and pointed to the baby. "We've come for that."

"You can't have him." She dug her fingers into the baby, causing him to cry out.

Lydia, don't. Simon wanted to shout, but he considered what the group would do with her if they discovered his relation to her.

Barabbas drew nearer. "Oh, but we can."

Lydia searched the face of each man until her eyes fell on him. "Simon?"

He straightened.

"Simon, it's me."

Simon didn't respond. He couldn't. It might risk both their lives.

Ignoring her pleas, Barabbas pressed himself closer to her. "Give us that child, and we'll let you go."

"I will not." Lydia took a step away, putting space between herself and Barabbas and moving closer to Simon.

"Then we'll have to take him." Barabbas nodded toward Simon.

Reaching out, Simon grabbed for the boy.

"No!" Lydia moved the baby out of his grasp. "Simon, listen to me."

Simon made another attempt, but missed.

"Please don't do this."

"Just give him what he wants." Simon growled at her, keeping his voice low so as not to raise suspicions with Barabbas.

"I can't do that." Lydia clung to the boy. "This is wrong. You know this is wrong."

"Enough!" Barabbas swung his arm, knocking the baby from Lydia's hands and catching her in the process.

The boy let out a terrible wail as he hit the ground.

Lydia scrambled to regain possession of the boy.

Barabbas snatched the boy's leg before she could reach him. He untangled the boy from the headcloth, exposing his naked form, and held him up.

The baby's cries grew louder.

"Don't hurt him!" Lydia sobbed. "Please don't hurt him."

Barabbas removed his dagger from his belt and held the blade to the boy's throat. "Let his fate be the fate of every Roman."

"No!" Lydia lunged at him, swiping at the blade.

Simon was frozen in his spot. If he tried to get between them, Barabbas would doubt his loyalty and confirm their relationship.

"Release him!" Lydia dug her fingernails into Barabbas' arms.

He dropped the boy and used both hands to tear Lydia from himself. "You're mad, woman!" He shoved her to the ground.

Lydia thudded hard against the dirt.

Simon felt his stomach drop at the sound of his sister's body slamming against the ground. He held his breath, waiting for her to move.

"Simon, take care of this mess." Barabbas turned away holding his arm.

The others followed their leader.

Simon moved toward the boy crying on the ground and kneeled beside him.

Rising, Lydia reached toward them. "I won't let them hurt you." She rose slowly, as if not trusting her legs. "I won't let them kill you, too."

Turning to face his sister, he saw a strange look in Lydia's eyes. This child was not hers, and yet she took on Barabbas to spare his life.

Simon turned his attention to the child. A strange glint came from the boy's watery eyes. Thoughts flashed and collided in his mind. With one slice, he could end this life and secure his place with Barabbas' group without another doubt. No one would miss this unwanted child.

He glanced at his sister, who struggled to move toward him. But someone did want the boy. Lydia wanted him more than his family had shown their desire for him. With options running low, he pulled out his dagger and scooped the child into his other hand.

"No!" Lydia lunged at him but missed.

Simon pointed his dagger at her. "Stop."

The threat caused her to hesitate.

Knowing the exact positioning, he moved the edge of his blade to the baby's thigh.

"Simon, don't." Lydia wept.

With a quick swipe, he cut into the baby's flesh and then dropped him.

The boy let out a terrible scream.

"Simon, how could you?" Lydia's question hung in the air.

Without answering her, he rose to his full height and fled.

CHAPTER 12

Shoving his dagger back into its place, Simon ran until he neared the gate. Tucking in with a large crowd, he cleared the entrance and headed toward the meeting house.

He stopped mid-stride. He couldn't go back. A flash of red went across his vision, accompanied by the haunting cries of the baby. He didn't complete the mission. Barabbas would find out.

Simon held his head as he tucked into a narrow alley.

Should he lie? Should he tell the truth? Neither would guarantee Barabbas' favor.

He turned toward the market street, blending into the flow of the crowd while he considered his options.

The wound he inflicted on the child wasn't fatal, but it could be without proper care. He floated from stall to stall, thoughtless of his direction. Lydia might take the child to the midwife who lives next to the potter. She'd help him.

A pile of plump pears caught his attention. He'd lived off meager supplies while waiting among the tombs and his stomach demanded to be filled. He purchased one of the larger pears and bit into the crisp flesh, savoring the sweet fruit.

The boy might die anyway, so if he told Barabbas the job was done, it might become true.

He sunk his teeth into the next bite.

What if Lydia told someone she saw him? What if word was spreading even now?

He glanced around and caught sight of a guard. Finishing off his pear and storing the center in his pouch, he headed for a nearby tunnel entrance.

With effortless movements, he retreated into a narrow street, sucked in a breath, and lowered himself into the waiting mouth.

Water splashed around him as he dropped. Simon pressed himself toward the walls, seeking as much high ground as he could manage.

He paced through the passage filtering through his options. There weren't many.

His stomach protested as he walked. The single pear had done little to quiet the beast in his midsection. He dug the core from his bag and held it up. Two years in the tunnels had taught him he could easily purchase a rat's loyalty.

Finding the largest nearby rodent, he held out the pear center.

The creature snatched it and ran away.

Hurrying to keep up, Simon followed the rat, hoping it would carry its feast to its nest. Unfortunately, the animal was too quick and he lost it around a corner. He swore under his breath and pressed his back against the curved wall.

He ran a shaking hand through his damp hair. "What am I going to do?"

Returning to the meeting house would mean facing Barabbas. Either having to admit he didn't kill the Roman child or that the woman who inflicted injury was his sister would cost him. Would either be worth the price?

He started through the tunnel again. What had the last few years gained him? Certainly not freedom. He hid among shadows and murders. Through all the spilled blood, he was no closer to seeing Rome purged from Israel than when he started. He abandoned kin for a group of men who would trade him for a handful of denarii if given the chance.

Trudging along, he took stock of his belongings. His money pouch contained merely two coins. He was supposed to earn more for each rock child he returned to Barabbas. The tunic on his back desperately needed a wash. He noticed his worn gray cloak could also benefit from a good scrub. He recently mended his sandals, though he knew the water and muck he traversed would wear them faster if he stayed in the tunnels. His curved dagger swayed against his body, the blade that had tasted of so much blood would at least provide protection and make a meal of anything he could catch.

He hesitated, realizing he was taking account in preparation. Returning to the meeting house would certainly lead to his end. Barabbas would punish him for his sister's actions, or worse. He couldn't go back. The leader would interpret his hesitation to kill a child as aligning with the traitors of Israel, despite the number of Roman lives he had taken.

The tunnels would provide shelter as long as he kept moving. He'd grown to know them better than the streets above. He would survive. He had to.

Simon wandered the underground system, venturing above only as often as he dared and only when he absolutely needed to do so. During the first few days, the rats unwillingly shared their food until it became scarce. Simon considered hunting them, but had no means of cooking the meat. Building a fire in the tunnels was unwise and building one above ground would attract unwanted attention.

After five days, he passed an opening and heard familiar sounds coming from above. The lively hum of activity signaled that many had emerged from their homes after the midday rest. His stomach pressed him upward. If he didn't find substance soon, he wouldn't be able to stay ahead of Barabbas and the others who might be seeking a reward for his return.

Emerging from an entrance, Simon kept to the shadows. The stench of the underground clung to his tunic and cloak. He needed to be quick so as not to draw too much attention to himself.

With the market crowded, he could take what he dared, but didn't want to risk being labeled a thief. If caught, he would surely bear the consequences of all his crimes.

Piles of fruit, mounds of spices, and bundles of grains called to him. If he could manage a few samples, he could gain some strength.

His vision blurred and his steps faltered. He swayed and tumbled forward, bumping into several people.

They cursed him and pushed him away, making comments about his smell and appearance.

Simon's midsection ached as he stumbled away from the market. Reaching out, he felt for the side of a building and slowly slid down it.

"Adonai, I have no right to speak Your name or ask Your aid." He folded against the stone. "I've defiled myself by shedding blood."

His dry lips parted with a song of David, "Save me, O Elohim. For the waters have come up to my neck." He put his head against the cool stone, mumbling more of the psalm to himself.

His breath slowed and his throat dried. "Answer me, O Lord, for your steadfast love is good; according to your abundant mercy, turn to me. Hide not your face from your servant, for I am in distress; make haste to answer me."

The surrounding light shifted to shadows.

His heavy eyelids lowered. "You know my reproach, and my shame and my dishonor…"

Somewhere above him, a raven cried out.

"Do you need help?"

A deep voice spoke above Simon. He flinched, fearing Barabbas had discovered him. Lifting a hand to shield his eyes, he squinted, trying to see the form against the sunlight shining behind the man. He dropped his hand when he realized the stranger was shorter and less muscular than the zealot leader. He groaned.

The man came closer. "You look like you could use some aid."

Simon heard rustling sounds, like the man was searching for something in a bag.

"I saw a peculiar raven flying above, cloaked in gray." The man looked up as if searching for the bird and dropped his gaze back down to Simon. "Like you."

Simon looked at his worn gray cloak.

The man knelt beside him. "You know the raven is an interesting creature. Adonai sent a flock to Elijah to care for him. You know this story, yes?"

Simon's mind was fuzzy.

"As I recall, the prophet wanted to die."

Simon heard more rustling.

"He found himself on the wrong side of popular opinion and a death sentence around his neck. Adonai told him to flee. Elijah found himself a place to hide in the wilderness by a brook. Can you believe his favor, a brook, in a drought no less?"

Simon smelled something familiar.

"You'd think the prophet would be grateful, but all he could do was complain about his lot. Well, Adonai told him to eat and sleep."

The smell grew stronger.

"Take it."

Simon opened his eyes to see a sizeable chunk of bread being thrust at him. He accepted the piece and shoved the whole thing into his mouth. The warmth of the freshly baked bread nestled inside his chest.

"Elijah obeyed, but when he woke, nothing had changed. He still felt the same about his circumstances." The man tore off a small piece of the loaf and popped it into his mouth. "So, Adonai told him to do it again. Eat and sleep." He broke another piece and held it out.

Simon snatched the bread and pressed it past his lips, chewing in haste.

"Elijah obeyed, same as before." The stranger held out a water skin.

Simon took the skin and lifted it to his cracked lips. A stream of water quenched the fire in his throat.

"Only this time, when Elijah woke, something had changed." He offered another piece of bread.

With each bite, Simon's vision cleared.

"Though his circumstances hadn't changed much. He was still a prophet on the run. His life was still in danger. He was still exiled to a remote area. The thing that had changed was Elijah. He was ready to move forward in obedience." He handed Simon another piece. "Adonai always provides."

Simon discovered enough strength to speak. "My mother says that."

The man held out the end of the loaf. "Mothers are wise about these things."

Simon took the last offering and devoured it in one bite.

CHAPTER 13

"Why are you doing this?"

"I'm glad you asked." The stranger smiled. "I heard a wise prophet share about a man who went down to Jericho—"

"Let me guess." Simon lifted himself against the wall. "The traveler fell among thieves."

"You've heard the same prophet?"

"I've heard the story." Simon groaned. "It was one of my brother's favorites to tell."

"He sounds wise."

"He used to be."

"What happened to him?"

Simon leaned his head against the stone. "The authorities sentenced him to death on a Roman cross."

"What was his crime?"

"Claiming to be the King of the Jews."

The man leaned forward. "You're a brother of Jesus of Nazareth?"

Simon squinted. "One of them."

"I've met your other brothers. James. Joseph. Jude."

"That's them."

"What are you doing out here in the streets? Have you not heard?"

"Heard what?"

"Your brother's not dead. He's risen."

Simon wiped his face. "Hopeful rumors."

"They're not rumors at all." The stranger settled beside Simon. "We've seen him. With our own eyes."

"Then you can bring me to him?"

He lowered his gaze. "I can't."

"Because he's still in the tomb."

"Because he was lifted into the clouds a few weeks after he rose." The man jumped to his feet. "Come, I will take you to the empty tomb." He held his hand out.

Simon grasped his forearm and pulled himself to his feet.

"What are you called, brother of Jesus?"

"Simon."

"Nicolaus." He put his hand on his chest. "Come with me."

The two pressed through the bustling city streets toward the gates. On the other side of the walls, Simon followed Nicolaus to a beautiful garden.

"There." Nicolaus pointed toward the edge of the garden.

Simon slowed his pace. Ahead lay an open tomb. "Whose is this?" He glanced at Nicolaus. "My poor family could not afford such luxury."

"Joseph of Arimathea." Nicolaus came alongside him. "A Pharisee, but a good man."

Simon shook his head. "Adonai provided a tomb at the hands of a Joseph." He placed his palm on the mouth of the opening. "Joseph was our father's name." He glanced back to Nicolaus over his shoulder. "We have no such extravagance in Nazareth."

Simon ducked to peer inside the cave. The inside was beautifully crafted. Whoever was commissioned for such work was an artist. The smooth surfaces and heavy scent of cut stone told Simon the work on the burial cave had been completed rather recently.

Small nooks were hewn into several sides of the cave, waiting to be filled. On one side there was a large opening where bodies would be prepared. Family members would leave the deceased on the rock shelf that resembled a table for a year to decompose before the bones were collected and placed into burial boxes. Boxes would then take up residence among the small recesses so family members could rest among their ancestors.

Simon took a shaking step inside. He slowly neared the table and ran his fingers across the smooth top. "Jesus lay here."

Nicolaus stepped inside. "Only for a few days."

"Is my brother truly risen?"

"Just as He said." Nicolaus chuckled. "One of the women claimed to see two messengers sitting here when they found the body gone."

"They?"

"Mary from Magdala and your mother." Nicolaus placed his palm on the empty table. "They came to anoint the body further and instead found Jesus risen."

"My mother was here?"

"She still is. She's with your siblings and your brother's followers."

For the last two years, Simon had pushed aside every thought and memory of his family. Martha had told him they stayed, but he assumed they'd eventually return to Nazareth. If they were in Jerusalem all this time, had they heard of his deeds? Tears fell, causing small, dark circles on the stone. "They're still in Jerusalem?"

"They've been staying with a priest in the city. In fact, tonight is the last night of a wedding feast for your brother Joseph. You should go to them."

"Joseph's getting married?" Simon's chest tightened. "I don't think they'd want to see me." He put his clenched fists on the table. "For the past few years, I've been used as an instrument of war."

"How so?"

"I joined a group of zealots and have been taking orders from Barabbas."

Nicolaus put his hand on Simon's shoulder. "Jesus called a man named Simon to follow him and he was a zealot when they met. He was hungry for Rome's removal. Your brother also selected a tax collector named Matthew, a man living on the spoils of Roman occupation. The two, though brutal enemies, lived and served together for three years. How do you think they did this?"

Simon's mind flashed with his multiple battles with Roman soldiers. "I'm not sure."

"Because Adonai can use any weapon He wants, any way He wants." He squeezed Simon's shoulder before releasing his grip. "We must be careful not to find fault with His tools."

"I've been a fool." Simon hung his head. "I've spent my whole life chasing honor and pride. I've run from my family, from Barabbas, from everyone and everything." He ran his fingers over the cold stone, sending a shiver up his arm. "Forgive me, brother. I don't want to run anymore." The chill in his arm was replaced by a warmth that started in his chest and spread outward. "Please, forgive me."

Nicolaus headed toward the opening. "I can take you to your family."

Fear and hope clashed with him at the idea. Would his simple family welcome him back or send him away after they found out all he'd done? There was only one way to know for sure.

Simon followed Nicolaus through the streets of Jerusalem toward the Upper City. As they neared a large villa, Simon heard instruments playing inside the house.

Nicolaus opened the wooden door and waved him in.

Simon stood frozen as the sounds of merriment and music encompassed him.

"Come in." Nicolaus waved again.

With shaking steps, Simon entered.

Flickers of oil lamps cast dancing shadows on the tall walls.

Simon made his way deeper into the villa and toward the feast. Passing through an archway, he first noticed Lydia across a room full of people. His heart squeezed as he saw the tiny bundle in her arms. He lifted his eyes to her face in time to see his name appear on her lips.

Before he could step toward her, James and Jude blocked his path.

James put his hands in front of Simon. "State your business."

Simon bowed his head. "I've come to seek shelter."

"Why?"

"Brother, I've done terrible things." Simon glanced around James to catch sight of Lydia. "Things I'm no longer proud of, and I would like to confess something."

Jude leaned to whisper in James' ear. "Should we trust him?"

"Please, you must let me speak!"

James gave a simple nod.

Simon pushed the hood of his cloak down. "I have blood on my hands. More than I've ever wanted, but for the past few days, I've been running." He turned pleading eyes on Lydia. "After the incident at the rocks, I couldn't return to my... group."

He cleared his throat. "I've hidden among the shadows of Jerusalem. At first, I didn't know what I was searching for or even what I would do on my own." He spread his hands. "When I was hungry and tired, I cried out to Adonai. I must have passed out or something because all I remember is a man's voice. He gave me food and shared with me about Jesus."

Simon chuckled. "He recounted lessons of my own brother." He shook his head slowly. "I lived with Jesus my whole life, and it took me getting to my lowest place and a stranger's kindness to have me realize the truth." He looked at James. "I know Jesus is Messiah." Tears filled his eyes. "I know it with every part of me. I've asked for forgiveness, but I need to ask for more."

He stepped toward Lydia, but James put his hand up again to stop him.

"It's alright." Lydia adjusted the baby in her arms. "Let him come."

James dropped his hand.

Simon took a few cautious steps. "I can't begin to apologize for my role in everything that has happened." He took another step toward her. "I never meant for you to get hurt. When I saw you on the ground—" His words caught in his throat. "It was one of the most sobering moments I've had in a long time." He looked at the babe. "I hope you realize why I had to do what I did."

Lydia dropped her gaze to the boy for a moment before her attention snapped back to him. "You had to injure him to spare him."

Simon nodded. "I had to show them the blood on my dagger so they wouldn't return to do the deed themselves."

"You saved him." Lydia crushed the baby against her chest. "Simon." She cleared the space between them and wrapped her brother with her free arm. "I knew you were still in there."

Simon buried his face in her hair. "It took you drawing me out." He stepped back. "And Jesus' forgiveness." He moved toward Nicolaus. "And you."

"I was on my way to care for a widow when I saw you lying in the street. So many others passed you by, but I couldn't." Nicolaus turned to Lydia. "I kept thinking, 'What would Jesus and Stephen do?'" He lifted a shoulder. "They would have stopped to feed him, so I did."

James came closer. "I'm glad you have returned, Simon, but I don't think you can stay here. Saul is—"

"Seeking me." Simon hung his head. "Because of my part in the death of the senator's daughter."

James came to his side. "The council has agreed to Saul's war."

"This isn't war, brother." Simon put a hand on James' shoulder. "War has rules. This is hunting."

"What can we do?"

Simon dropped his hand. "Prey only has one choice; hide or die."

James shook his head. "Saul is making it nearly impossible to hide in Jerusalem."

Simon looked into the faces of his siblings. "Then we must flee."

"Where?" James put his hand to his head. "We have so many here in Jerusalem who depend on us. Widows. New believers. We can't just abandon them."

"We can't stay together either. It's too dangerous."

"At least Saul seems content to hunt within the city and Assia is safe in Nazareth."

"Saul is a hungry predator." Simon shook his head. "I don't think his hunting grounds will remain contained for long. Especially not if the Way spreads beyond Jerusalem. His hunger will not be satisfied until he has captured every last one of us. Mark my words." His breath came in ragged bursts. "Vengeance has a way of consuming those who seek it."

CHAPTER 14

Simon looked at each of his brothers, putting certainty to his words.

James pressed his temple. "Should we send you to Nazareth?"

"I don't want to draw attention to our family there."

Lydia moved into the circle. "What about Damascus?"

Simon tilted his head. "Damascus?"

James nodded. "We have friends there. Fellow Way Followers who might hide you until we can deal with Saul." He looked at Lydia. "If nothing else, at least Simon could warn Ananias about what might be coming his way. He might be the one to provide us with aid this time." He turned to Simon. "We can send a messenger to him to see if he's willing."

Simon gazed around the gathering. "What about Ima and the girls?"

Mary came between James and Jude. "I'm staying with John."

James groaned. "Ima."

"Jesus put John in charge of me for good reason." Mary folded her arms. "I have to keep my faith in His choice."

Simon turned to his youngest sister. "Salome?"

James spoke before she could answer. "I can send her back to Nazareth."

Lydia chuckled. "I think you'd have an easier time commanding the waves. Ever since that fiery tongue licked her head, she's been an unstoppable sandstorm. I don't think you could make her do anything, even if you tied her to a camel." She glanced in Salome's direction.

"Saul doesn't scare me." Salome stuck out her chest. "My big brother can handle him."

Simon glanced to Lydia. "Fiery tongue?"

Salome chuckled. "We have much to catch you up on, brother."

"I'd say so." Simon looked to the baby in Lydia's arms. "And you two?"

Lydia shifted her attention to Nicolaus. "I have an offer of marriage." She inclined her head toward him. "If he's willing to take a widow and an orphan as his own, I will go where he leads."

A warm sense of familiarity and comfort crawled inside Simon's heart. It had been too long since he was surrounded by family. In the middle of a feast, he stepped back into his position as if he'd never left.

As his gaze moved toward the baby in his sister's arms, another feeling shadowed his happiness. Fear mingled with the sounds of wedding music. He ran a shaking hand through his hair. He couldn't stay. Even as much as the wholeness he felt started to chip away some of the guilt and shame he carried, his presence posed too much danger to the people he cared about.

He cleared his throat to cover the tightness clawing at him. "When can you send a messenger?"

James lifted an eyebrow. "In the morning, I suppose. We should get an answer back in a few weeks' time."

Time. The word rolled through Simon. Out of all the things he didn't possess, time was the greatest.

The start of another cheerful song called them back to the wedding feast.

While the others returned to their song, dance, and feast, Simon watched them like they were actors in a Greek play. He kept his distance as an audience member, smiling but not breaking the boundary between actor and audience. If he joined his siblings on stage, he'd only bring more tragedy to their comedy.

Feasting stretched into the night as if everyone present knew the end of the celebration would awaken them to the reality of their circumstances.

The following morning, Simon stood in the courtyard of the villa listening to Peter share about Jesus. It'd been years since he felt the enveloping sense of community as those around him sang the psalms of David.

Simon felt a shift next to him. He turned to see a large man with a similar structure and scars to Barabbas. A tremor went through him as his body recalled the training under his former leader.

"Don't believe we've met." The man inclined his head in an informal bow. "I'm Hiram."

"Simon."

"The lost sheep."

Simon lifted a brow.

"You're the lost sibling the others have spoken of."

"You know my brothers and sisters?"

Hiram indicated with his chin across the room. "James' wife Elissa is my oldest friend. She and I grew up together."

Simon's gaze drifted to the young woman with a young one on her hip who stood next to his older brother. "I seem to have missed much while I've been away." He turned back to Hiram. "I returned only last night."

"I've been gone for some time as well."

"For your trade?"

"No." Hiram crossed his arms over his chest. "I didn't agree with some of James' choices."

Simon watched Hiram's arms tense. He had fled under similar circumstances.

"No matter." Hiram shook his head. "It appears Adonai has returned us both to the fold."

Simon nodded.

"Lydia tells me she's going to Rabbi Ethan's after this to have her baby circumcised and pledge her marriage vows to Nicolaus."

"Why is she in such a hurry? She's still obviously mourning her last betrothed." Simon let his gaze drift toward Lydia and her dark-colored tunic, recalling all the missed events his siblings shared during the night of feasting. He still couldn't believe his own sister was the betrothed of the man who Saul consented to be murdered or that she had been the one to purchase the young Pharisee's death for revenge. Simon and Lydia had spent much of the night discussing their twisted paths.

"Nicolaus found a caravan heading toward Antioch." Hiram nodded toward Nicolaus. "I guess he thought it best to leave Jerusalem and put as much distance between them and Saul as they can manage."

"Why Antioch?"

"Nicolaus has family there." He lifted one shoulder. "Guess anywhere that's not Jerusalem is safer."

Safe. The word dripped with false hope in Simon's ears. Would any of them be safe with Saul on the prowl?

Simon consented to stand witness with the others to the rituals of Lydia and her child and participated in bidding them farewell. Once they were gone, he sought James. "Brother, may I have a word?"

"Of course." James waved toward an empty room in the villa.

Simon followed him inside, appreciating the privacy among a house packed with people. "I want to express my regret once more for taking off." He peered up at his brother under lowered brows. "I was young and stupid. I believed the lies of the zealots and felt their cause was just. Honestly, I wanted much more than justice. I was seeking revenge, and it didn't satisfy."

"And now?"

"Now, I feel lost." Simon felt a weight in his chest. "Staying in Jerusalem doesn't feel right, but neither does running away again."

"Have you prayed about this?"

Simon nodded. "Adonai remains as silent as the grave."

James walked across the room and rummaged through a stack of belongings. He retrieved a pouch and brought it to Simon. "Here."

"What's this?"

"A few coins." He held it out. "I noticed you took some of mine last time."

A pang of guilt struck between Simon's ribs. "You discovered that?"

James smiled. "If there was one thing Abba taught me, it was to keep count of my coins." He grabbed Simon's hand and shoved the pouch into his palm. "I want you to have this for your journey to Damascus. It's not much, but it'll help."

"Do you really think Damascus is the right place for me?"

James lifted a shoulder. "I've sent word to Ananias, so you have some time to seek Adonai. But just in case," he pointed to the pouch, "you'll have that and my prayers."

For the next two days, Simon wandered the priest's villa and prayed. He spent time with his mother and siblings and even played with his nephew, Joshua. He partook in meetings with Jesus' followers but didn't add to the conversations.

When Peter suggested Simon take Nicolaus' place among the seven, James intervened. Without going into deep explanations, James revealed Simon's plans to leave Jerusalem soon. Simon was grateful for his older brother's leadership and guidance. Yet, he still wasn't sure if Damascus was the place he needed to head.

As evening approached, Hiram stormed into the villa. "James!"

Simon met him in the open courtyard. "James is not back yet."

"I need to speak to him at once."

"I'm sure they'll return any moment." Simon watched a vein pulse on the side of Hiram's neck. "Anything I can assist you with?"

Hiram fixed steely eyes on Simon. "No offense intended, but I need to talk to the leader of this little collection."

"Something happened?"

Hiram glanced across the room.

Simon followed his gaze and noticed his mother and Salome appear from the kitchen.

"I just came from the market and heard the rumors." Hiram lowered his voice and growled in a guttural tone. "The council has given Saul full permission to arrest Way Followers."

Simon swallowed hard.

Hiram set a hard stare on Simon. "Men and women." He shifted his gaze back to the two women.

Simon's chest tightened looking at Salome and his mother. If Saul was allowed to hunt women, it would only be a matter of time before their entire family was sharing a cell. Simon had to get out of Jerusalem as soon as possible. For their sake and his.

CHAPTER 15

Simon pressed against a stone wall, digging his fingers into the rough grooves. His heart pounded as he fought to gain control of his breath. The familiar cloak of darkness draped over him bringing an unusual sensation.

It was not the shadows he feared, for they had been his constant companions for the last three years. As the chill of coming night brushed against his cheeks, the tide of his life shifted. Tonight, he was no longer the hunter, he was the prey.

He was not afraid of death; no zealot could be. Death would come for him as it had come for every man before him. The dread that quaked his bones was knowing if death came this night, he would go to Sheol as a coward. No honor. No pride. Not even with his head held high.

He'd run so many times in his life and tonight he'd do it again. This time was different. He wasn't running away only for himself, but to protect his family from the danger that was hunting him.

The hues above him shifted. Sunset signaled the closing of the gates. Sounds of metal groaning and wood creaking echoed down the street. The city gates shut like the snap of the great fish's teeth around Jonah. Simon was trapped in Jerusalem like the prophet in the beast's belly.

If he showed himself to the guards, they might recognize him. They'd sooner open a cell door for him than one of the city gates. Simon carried knowledge of Barabbas' victims and blood on his own hands. If Rome captured him, there was a chance those secrets would come to light. It was a risk Simon knew Barabbas wasn't eager to take, as the Romans would be unlikely to free the murderous zealot leader a second time.

If Simon was going to make it out of Jerusalem alive, he'd have to find another path. Thankfully, the gates were not the only way out of the heavily guarded city.

He allowed his gaze to travel upwards. The walls of Jerusalem were too tall to scale alone. Dropping his gaze, the allure of the tunnels called to him. A network of underground passageways provided for movement below the surface. There were entrances hidden in plain sight, and Simon knew of one in the next alley over.

The tunnels were his best choice for escape, but they wouldn't be empty. There was a strong chance he'd cross paths with someone from his former throng. They'd drag him right back to Barabbas and he would certainly meet death this night.

He glanced to his right, searching the encroaching darkness for any sign of movement. Few people remained in the dusty streets after the closing of the gates. Simon concealed himself among the shadows, watching as the occasional man shuffled by and a group of Roman guards patrolled the area.

When a momentary break in the patrol came, Simon pulled the hood of his gray cloak over his head and hurried toward the tunnel entrance. He slipped through the narrow alley and found the opening.

With one last breath of fresh air, he ducked into the darkness below and was immediately welcomed by the stench of the underground. The foul smells of refuse, standing water, and stale air hit him all at once.

He breathed through gritted teeth as he had trained himself, giving his nose time to adjust. Keeping to the walls, he hoped the darkness they provided would be enough to hide him. His worn sandals splashed muddy water as he trotted through puddles, disturbing the silhouette of his shadow. The constant drip of distant water echoed against the concave walls and short ceilings. He timed his steps with the rhythm, attempting to mask his presence further.

During his time with Barabbas, he hunted those whose bodies flowed with Roman blood and any who sympathized by their compliance. His curved dagger still hung inside his cloak, stained with his choices. He'd given much for a mere taste of victory. A taste that had soured his soul.

His former zealous companions counted it noble to die spitting in the face of foreign authorities. They walked in the path of the Hasmoneans who chose death instead of foreign rule. Simon's own brother had chosen death instead of dismantling Rome. It had taken Simon too long to realize martyrdom solved nothing and now death loomed over him like the last plague over Egypt.

Barabbas wasn't the only man hunting him. Somewhere among the limestone houses and winding streets above was Saul. Another man hungry for Simon's blood. A life for a life. By all accounts, a fair end. Blood had been shed at Simon's hand and so blood must be repaid.

If Simon could reach the northernmost point of the tunnel system, it would put him on the other side of the Fish Gate and outside Jerusalem. While there were no cities of refuge, as in the days of his ancestors, there was a promise. Damascus. James had sent word ahead to Ananias, but Simon didn't have time to wait for a reply. He needed to flee Jerusalem before he found himself on the wrong end of a dagger or a pile of stones.

The difficulty Simon faced was the same for one fleeing to a refuge city, getting there alive. In the time of Joshua, an innocent slayer could flee to one of the six designated cities for safety. As he pressed on through the tunnels, he was fully aware of one major difference between himself and those who fled to the old refuge cities; Simon wasn't innocent.

At each intersection of the tunnels, Simon hesitated. He slowly checked around the corner before scurrying across like a rodent.

He recalled his first time in the passageways. The filthy creatures who shared the underground roads startled him with their quick movements and nasty demeanor. It didn't take long for Simon to learn they could also lead to food and fresh water. Even with several rats scurrying along the walls tonight, he couldn't stop to follow them.

If he made it out of Jerusalem, Damascus was at least a nine-day journey on foot. Simon wasn't sure if he'd make it. The only solace he had was that both Saul and Barabbas were yet unaware of his destination. A reprieve Simon hoped continued.

Damascus was as vast and populated as Jerusalem, and far away from the authority of the council. There were no more refuge cities, but since Damascus was under Syrian control, it held the potential to become Simon's stronghold.

The pathway ahead of him twisted and turned until it finally came to an end just outside the city. Reaching the mouth of the opening, Simon inhaled deeply, filling his lungs with fresh air and temporary freedom. He made it out of Jerusalem, but he still had a long way to go.

Jericho was his first aim. If he traveled all night, he'd make it by sunrise. That was his plan; travel under the cover of night to the nearest city and find a place to sleep through the day. It was the opposite of what he'd been taught growing up, as well as to never travel alone. He was breaking both guidelines this trip.

He knew his brothers would have offered to escort him to Damascus, but the yoke that weighed on his shoulders was his alone to bear. He would allow no one else to come to harm because of his choices. That's why he was leaving without telling any of them, just as he had done before.

Without so much as a backward glance to Jerusalem, he continued north. Looking back would do nothing but slow him down. He would take the advice the divine messenger gave to Lot and his family, "Escape for your life. Do not look back or stop anywhere in the valley. Escape to the hills, lest you be swept away."

The trek from Jerusalem to Jericho was long and difficult. With the drastic elevation changes, the road to Jericho was as dangerous as it was rough. The path was made all the more difficult by thieves looking for opportunities presented by weary travelers. Thankfully, years of training gave Simon courage to make the journey alone. His curved blade and sharpened skills would ward off any man who dare to cross him.

Simon made it to Jericho as the city gates were opening with the breaking of a new day. His legs felt as heavy as his eyelids and his stomach protested its vacancy.

He let his ample nose lead him toward the market street. There, he selected fruit, nuts, and freshly baked bread. He ate as he walked, inquiring of the tradesmen for a place to lay his head. They directed him to a nearby inn.

With a small room secured for the day, Simon washed the dust from his face and feet before settling down to sleep. He knew pitching a tent in the wilderness was far cheaper, but he left without proper supplies and found it easier to hide among crowds than in the vastness of plains. His years as a zealot had taught him how to become a shadow, and that the easiest place to hide was in plain sight.

CHAPTER 16

After four nights traveling along the Jordan River Valley, Simon came upon the southern tip of the Sea of Galilee. The familiar waters shimmered in the moonlight. He had plenty of time to make it to Tiberias before the rising sun. There, he would find a place to rest before starting east toward Damascus.

Staring at the water's surface, he took note of his dim reflection. He was never one for vanity, but the certainty that he'd never watch his hair gray caused him to pause. Adonai had seen him halfway through his journey. How much further would that favor go?

Standing at the edge of the shore, he heard a faint whisper to the west. Home. Nazareth was not far, but it was in the opposite direction. He glanced behind himself for the first time in five days. There was no sign of anyone following him. He'd been so careful, never sharing his real name, dipping into a city just as the gates were opening, and sneaking out just before the gates closed for the night.

His journey was half over, and Damascus would soon be within reach.

But the pull of home called to him again. Yielding to the choice would add at least a day to his journey, if not more. His oldest sister's face flashed in his mind's eye. Assia would welcome him like a victor at the Greek Games. Truly, his family should be mourning him, not offering up a fatted calf.

If Damascus was to be his city of refuge, this might be the last time he saw family. Assia's cheeks were the only ones he did not kiss before he left Jerusalem. If he went to Nazareth, would it draw unwanted attention to her family?

Simon glanced to the northeast, the direction he should continue. He huffed and pointed his feet west. Lifting a silent plea, he begged Adonai that this diversion would not cost him anything more than time.

The small village of Nazareth came into view with the rising sun. Simon saw the line of women waiting at the well and caught a glimpse of a familiar form. He hesitated as he watched his sister chat with the other women. At that moment, he knew he could walk away, and she'd never know he was that close. Assia was happy and safe. Would his presence change all that?

In that thought, Assia's glance caught him. She put down her water jug and ran toward him at a full sprint.

Simon opened his arms to catch his sister as she slammed into him.

"Simon."

Her breath was warm against his ear and he smelled the familiar smells of earth and life on her.

"Oh, Simon. I thought I'd never see you again." Assia pulled herself far enough away to put space between their faces, but kept her arms around his neck. "Where have you been? I've been so worried about you."

"It's a long story." Simon's eyes traveled away from hers. Noticing her slightly protruding midsection, he recalled James' mention of the birth of her first child while he was away. He put her down gently and motioned to her stomach. "Another one?"

"Oh, yes." She placed both hands on her middle. "Hiskiel is so pleased." Her smile widened. "We're praying for a little brother for Hadassah."

"I remember a big sister once saying how much trouble little brothers were." He watched Assia's cheeks bloom.

"Most of them are." She lifted a brow with the tease. "That doesn't mean they're any less loved."

"Where's my little niece?" Simon looked around. "James told me all about her."

"She's home." Assia started back to the line for water. "It's been hard to pry her out of Devora's hands since we returned home."

Simon followed her to the small well. "Hiskiel's sister-in-law has her own children, does she not?"

"Hers are so big that they run all over the house." Assia collected her jug and set it on her hip. "Devora misses the days when they were little and she could just hold them." She stepped back into the line. "They've been trying to have another. In the meantime, she's making up for it by holding onto Hadassah for as long as possible."

Simon let a comfortable silence engulf the space between them as Assia waited patiently for her turn.

After drawing her water, Assia headed away.

Simon attempted to match her slower pace.

"Did you meet your nephew?"

The memory of the feeling of his dagger in the leg of Lydia's child flipped his stomach. He swallowed hard.

"Doesn't Joshua look so much like James?"

"Joshua?" Simon shook his head to clear his vision. "Oh, yes. He does. I thought you meant Stephen."

"Stephen?" Assia hesitated. "Why would I be referring to Lydia's betrothed?"

Simon stopped. "You don't know?"

"Know what?"

"About Lydia and Stephen." Simon looked toward the south. "They left two days before me. I thought they would have visited you on their way to Antioch."

"Antioch?" The word came out in a high tone. "Why would they be traveling to Antioch?"

"That's where Nicolaus is from."

"Nicolaus? What does he have to do with any of this?"

"This doesn't make any sense." Simon rubbed the back of his neck. "Why wouldn't Lydia stop here with Stephen and Nicolaus? I'm sure they would have."

"I've been waiting on word of their marriage." Assia slowed. "Why would they be traveling with Nicolaus?"

"You truly haven't heard?"

"What?" Assia's voice boarded on panic. "Tell me."

"Stephen's dead."

"No." She shook her head. "You said he was traveling with Lydia."

"Lydia named her son Stephen."

"Her son?" Assia's hand flew to her forehead. "But she and Stephen never…"

"The baby was an abandoned Roman. Lydia found him and adopted him. She married Nicolaus and he was taking her away from Jerusalem, back to his home in Antioch."

"Why would Lydia marry Nicolaus? What happened?"

"Assia." Simon stepped in front of her. "Stephen was stoned to death for teaching about Jesus in his synagogue."

Assia's fingers slipped from her jar.

Simon caught the vessel before it collided with the ground. He extended his other hand to steady his sister, who appeared ready to faint. "Maybe you should rest a moment."

"I don't want rest." She swatted his arm. "I want you to tell me everything right this moment."

"Let's get you home." Simon kept his arm around her waist to assist her. "I'll tell you what I know."

Simon steadied the water jug in one hand and his sister in the other as they walked. He recounted everything he'd been told of Stephen's stoning and then shared Lydia's discovery of the rock child and her hurried marriage to Nicolaus.

By the time they reached the house of Elidad, Assia was stable once more. "Poor Lydia. I can't imagine what she's been through."

Simon placed the water jug on the half wall of the small courtyard. He felt a twinge of guilt, having kept back some of the bigger truths he was not yet ready to share with his oldest sister.

Assia hugged her midsection. "I've been eagerly waiting to hear that Lydia wed, and instead she's become a widow, mother, and wife all in a matter of weeks."

The urge to reveal more parted Simon's lips. Before he could release the words, a voice called from the dirt road.

"Assia!"

Simon turned to see Lydia carrying baby Stephen and Nicolaus escorting a donkey and goat.

"Lydia!" Assia rushed toward her, enveloping her sister and nephew.

Nicolaus continued toward Simon, releasing the two animals into the courtyard. "Didn't think we'd run into you."

The accusation twisted like a blade in Simon's side, though he wasn't sure if there was malicious intent behind Nicolaus' words. "I thought you three would be well past Nazareth by now."

"We were supposed to be." Nicolaus began to unload the pack animal. "The caravan we were with had some struggles in the valley. Broken wagon wheels, injuries, and a hunt for a lost child all slowed us down." He wiped sweat from his brow. "Lydia convinced me a stop here would do us good before heading to Antioch." He flicked his gaze to the sisters. "I think she missed her family more than she realized she would."

Simon would never admit it out loud, but Assia's hug had warmed his soul.

"How long are you planning on staying?"

Simon mulled over the question. "This was an unplanned detour. I simply wanted to see Assia before continuing."

"Well," Nicolaus patted his donkey's neck, "I'm sure the girls won't let you leave without a good meal first."

The man who barely knew his sisters had spoken truth. Assia would sooner tie him down than allow him to walk away with an empty stomach. Catching his sisters' approach, he whispered to Nicolaus, "I haven't told Assia about Saul yet."

Nicolaus' brow lifted, but he spoke no words.

"I only just informed her of Stephen's death."

Nicolaus' brow settled with a simple nod. "It sounds like a family conversation is in order."

Another spoken truth Simon was dreading.

CHAPTER 17

Simon kept to the rear as Assia led the group inside the home and introduced Lydia's new family to her husband's family.

The women fawned over baby Stephen and his unique eyes.

Devora happily exchanged Hadassah for the younger infant, surrendering the girl to Assia's arms and smothering baby Stephen with kisses.

With Hadassah on her hip, Assia made her way to Simon and introduced him to his niece.

Simon evaluated the girl whose features mirrored more of her father, but her bright eyes were all her mother's. "She's beautiful."

"Well, I certainly think so." Assia kissed her daughter's head.

"Is there somewhere we can talk? Just me, you, and Lydia? There's something I need you to be aware of."

The appraising stare of his sister revealed her concerns, even if her words did not. "Let me get Hadassah settled and I'll meet you in the courtyard."

Escaping the sounds of life inside the house, Simon retreated outside. He paced the enclosed space until Assia and Lydia joined him.

Lydia wrapped her arms around him before he could say a word. "It's good to see you."

Simon allowed the moment of comfort before pulling away. "I honestly didn't think I'd see you again. It's favor that we happened to both be in Nazareth at the same time."

"We shall feast your company." Assia beamed.

"I have no time for feasts." Simon shook his head. "And neither does Lydia."

Lydia shot a glance at Assia. "I'm afraid Simon's right."

Assia crossed her arms over her chest. "What are you two not telling me?"

"I'm on the run from Saul." Simon hung his head. "I had to leave Jerusalem and I'm headed…" He slowly lifted his eyes. "Perhaps it best I don't share."

Assia moved her gaze to Lydia. "And you? Are you on the run too?"

Lydia nodded. "From Saul as well."

"What could the two of you possibly have done to rile such bloodlust from the same man?"

Simon glanced at Lydia.

Her lips disappeared into a thin line.

His attention returned to Assia. "Knowing might put you in danger."

Assia studied them for a few moments.

Lydia hung her head. "You might also think less of us if we told you."

"I see." Assia rolled a small stone with her foot. "We're keeping secrets in this family now."

Simon stepped toward her. "Assia—"

"No, no." She held up an open hand to him. "I understand."

"But, sister, you don't." Lydia closed the gap between the three of them. "We're talking about..." she lowered her voice, "...murder."

Assia's eyes grew wide.

Simon watched large tears roll down Lydia's face. "It's best not to say more." He looked at Assia. "Both of us coming here has put you in danger. As much as we've tried to leave our trouble in Jerusalem, I don't think it's going to stay there."

Lydia sniffed.

Simon kissed Lydia's damp cheeks, then Assia's. "I'm heading out."

"Wait." Assia caught his arm. "Let me at least get you some supplies. I won't let you leave without filling your belly and your pack."

One side of Simon's mouth raised. He knew his sister. "Make it quick."

Assia hurried inside.

Lydia wiped her face. "At least tell me what direction you're heading?"

Simon hesitated. "East."

"Passing by Capernaum?"

He nodded.

"Make sure to stop and see Zebedee. His family has been good to ours. I'm sure he will give you aid."

Simon recalled the old fisherman whose entire family became dedicated to Jesus early in his ministry. "Perhaps."

Assia returned with a full sack and a large tied bundle. "Here." She shoved the items at Simon. "Food for the trip and as many supplies as I could grab."

He received the offerings and tucked the bundle of food into his nearly empty pack.

"You're sure you can't stay?"

Simon noticed her eyes shimmering with unshed tears. "I shouldn't have come in the first place."

"I'm glad you did." Assia wrapped her arms around him. "May Adonai make His face shine upon you."

"And you." He held on to her for several moments before releasing her and exchanging her for Lydia. As he pulled her close, he whispered, "Don't stay too long. I don't want you anywhere near here if Saul heads this way."

She nodded against his neck. "Take care of yourself."

Simon released her and started away. He got only two steps before he turned back. Digging through his bag, he produced a piece of leather and held it out to Assia.

She accepted the gift. "What's this?"

"My sling." Simon gestured to her stomach. "For the boy. Ima gave it to me before I left Jerusalem. I've repaired it as much as I'm able."

Assia rubbed the worn leather. "It's beautiful."

"I figured every little boy needs a good sling." He paused. "Perhaps you can even tell him about me."

"What if the child is a girl?"

He shrugged. "Then teach her how to use it well."

She held the sling to her chest. "Thank you, Simon."

He turned away and headed down the dirt road leading out of Nazareth. Before leaving the town limits, Simon stopped at his family's home. James told him it had been sold to another family, but he couldn't help one last look at the old dwelling.

The sounds of his memories played while he stared at the small building. It was here his life started, and this would probably be the last time he'd see it. He couldn't help but feel the irony of his previous desires to never step foot on this ground and his aching desire to run inside and return to simpler days.

Leaving Nazareth, he traveled east until he grew too tired to walk and pitched a tent with the supplies from Assia. His sleep was restless and short. Instead of wasting time attempting more, he rose, packed, and continued.

Traveling further, he came to Capernaum and took Lydia's advice to seek Zebedee. The fishing village was not much bigger than Nazareth, but its homes were built from black basalt stones. Having spent time in town with Jesus when he relocated the family there, Simon knew the exact house belonging to Zebedee.

He approached the open door. "Greetings to the owner of this house."

An older woman appeared in the space and squinted at him. "Simon?"

"Hello, Salome. Is your husband here?"

"Come, come." She moved to wave him inside. "Zebedee."

The older fisherman shuffled from a back room. "Simon, my boy. Look at you."

"Shalom, my friend."

Zebedee put a hand on Simon's shoulder. "We haven't seen you in some time. How's your family?"

Simon swallowed hard. "Mostly well."

"To what do we owe this visit?" He dropped his hand and moved to recline at the low table. "How are my boys?"

"James and John are well and still ministering in Jerusalem."

"Fine. Fine." He motioned toward pillows next to the low table.

Simon settled on one.

"I miss those boys." Zebedee reclined at the head of the table. "Yet, I know they're doing Adonai's will."

"How's the fishing?"

"Not bad." Zebedee rubbed his gray-bearded chin. "I mostly hire out my boats these days." He studied

Simon from under white eyebrows. "You didn't say the reason for your visit. Did James send you?"

"No." Simon weighed the truth with protecting another family. "I'm simply traveling through and thought I'd ask for lodging."

The old fisherman's countenance shifted from curious to relief. "For a brother of our Lord? Of course. Stay as long as you wish."

"I appreciate the hospitality, but I'll only need the night. I'm eager to move on."

"I see."

Salome stood behind her husband. "I'll fix you up a place and a warm meal."

"While you do that," Zebedee rose, "I'm going to take Simon here on a little walk." He patted Simon's shoulder as he passed.

Simon followed the man out of the house and down the street as Zebedee ambled toward the edge of town that overlooked the Sea of Galilee. The wind coming off the water tousled Simon's dark hair.

"I don't know what kind of trouble you're in, Simon." Zebedee faced the sea. "But I'm old enough to read people as easy as scrolls. So, I'll ask this; are my boys safe?"

Simon's throat burned. He wasn't sure. The two sons of thunder were secure when he left, but he could not guarantee their condition would stay that way with Saul seeking revenge. How much truth should he share with the old man?

"If I have to repeat my question, I'll know the answer."

Simon heard the urgency in Zebedee's tone. "As far as I know, James and John are safe with my brothers and the others."

"But something's happened?"

"Yes."

"Are they involved?"

"No."

He nodded and asked nothing else.

After a few more quiet moments by the sea, Zebedee turned and headed toward his home.

Simon watched the water and the fishing boats a little longer before retiring to the house of the fisherman. He filled his stomach with Salome's offerings and slept until first light. Instead of staying for a parting, he simply left the borrowed sleeping mat rolled up and placed against the wall.

CHAPTER 18

The Via Maris route kept Simon traveling north. He stopped in Caesarea Philippi for his last day of rest in a city before heading east toward Damascus. After two days in the wilderness, the beautiful city finally crested over the horizon.

Simon hesitated at the sight of the impressive southern gate. The large archway welcomed him as indifferently as it did all those who passed through it. To any other, Damascus was simply a city to dwell and visit. For Simon, it would become his refuge.

He adjusted his packs, taking in the guards at the gate. His appearance was known in Jerusalem. What would these city guards think of him? He lifted his hood to mask his face and stepped into a caravan marching into the city. The group was large and diverse enough that he could blend in easily. All he had to do was pass through the gate and find Ananias.

Syrian guards stopped the occasional traveler, asking questions and searching wagons. This was a common sight for a city on the path of several trade routes. Damascus was like the center point of a spider's web with several strings traveling in different directions. It was one of many reasons Simon finally agreed with the James' suggestion to find shelter inside its walls.

Searches were to be expected when entering larger cities. The smaller cities were easier to enter, but harder to hide in. Larger cities were harder to enter, but one could melt into the crowds far more simply.

Simon pressed his dagger closer to his body, though it was already well concealed in the folds of his tunics. Of that, he had made sure. If the guards didn't recognize his countenance, they'd be sure to recognize the curved blade favored by those zealous against Rome.

He slouched his shoulders in an attempt to match the stature of the impatient and weary members of the caravan. The closer he came to the gate, the more control it took for his eyes to remain forward instead of searching to and fro.

When a guard stopped the couple in front of him, Simon breathed a sigh of relief. He shifted to move around them, until he heard a guard call after him.

"Halt."

Everything in him told him to run, but he knew running would only gain suspicion. The simplest way to blend in was to comply. He stopped mid-stride and waited.

The guard came close. "Have you any papers?"

Simon bowed low enough so the man could not see directly into his face and shook his head.

"State your business, Hebrew."

"Merely passing through." Simon watched the guard shift his weight from one sandaled foot to the other. A sign the man was making a choice.

"Let's see your bag."

Simon lowered his satchel and held it out.

The guard tipped over the bag, dumping the items onto the ground, and kicked several things around.

Heat rose on the sides of Simon's face. His hand eased toward the hilt of his dagger.

"What else are you carrying?"

Simon's hand froze. He knew he shouldn't have moved toward his weapon. The unconscious action had revealed more to the guard than he wanted.

The guard's hand wrapped around Simon's arm. "Let's have it."

Before Simon could think, his free hand was on his dagger.

"Enough!" a voice called through the crowd.

The guard turned toward the sound.

In the moment of opportunity, Simon knew he could withdraw his dagger, stab the guard in just the right spot, and flee his grasp before the man hit the ground.

But the one who had cried out rushed toward them and addressed the guard by name. "Jamal, release him at once."

"Ananias, you know this man?"

Simon felt the guard's grip tighten with the accusation.

Ananias stood beside Simon. "He's my guest. I would kindly ask you to remove your hand from his arm."

Jamal complied.

Simon released the hold on his dagger and let his hand drop to his side.

"My apologies." The guard bowed to Ananias. "I didn't know."

"Come, Simon." Ananias walked away.

Simon quickly shoved his scattered belongings back into his sack and hurried after the older man.

Ananias didn't say another word until they entered his dwelling. He shut the door, latched it, then turned to Simon. "What were you thinking?"

The sting of his words hit Simon like a child being rebuked by a parent.

"Your brother risked everything to send you to me and you pick a fight with a guard before you're even inside the gate?"

"I didn't start that fight."

"Ah." Ananias flicked his hand in the air. "It matters not."

"How'd you know I'd be at the gate today?"

"I didn't."

"How did you recognize me?"

Ananias moved deeper into the house. "I've been at the gate every morning since I received James' messenger. And you look a lot like your brothers. I didn't know I needed to look out for a trouble maker."

Simon trailed behind him, but hesitated at the archway.

Four women filled the room, each busy with their tasks. On the far end, an older woman washed bowls while two others sat on the floor beside her, kneading dough.

Simon's gaze traveled to the fourth, who sat alone next to a low table. She was much younger than the others and kept her head down while chopping vegetables. From the side view, Simon noticed her darker coloring and long eyelashes that almost kissed her cheeks when she blinked.

Ananias plucked two stone cups from a counter and slammed them onto a low table.

Simon's attention jumped to the older man. He watched Ananias pour liquid into the cups from a small jug.

"Drink."

Simon stepped toward the table and lifted one cup to his lips. The overly diluted wine made his stomach sour. "Got anything stronger?"

"Romans drink to forget." He lifted the second cup to his lips and emptied it. "We should strive to be better."

Simon caught sight of the young girl at the table, the left corner of her mouth raised and then dropped. It was clear that she found the old man's proverb amusing.

"Oh." Ananias put his cup down. "I didn't make introductions." He motioned to the older woman. "Simon, this is my wife, Mariah." His arm lowered to the two women on the floor. "My daughters-in-law, Eliana and Batya." He waved to the girl at the table. "And my daughter, Rachel."

"Shalom." Simon bowed toward them.

The four women paused only long enough to return the greeting.

Simon kept his eyes on Rachel. She seemed to embody her namesake; the beloved bride of Jacob.

"James tells me you have quite a story."

Ananias' words drew Simon's attention away. He stared at the man for a few moments, considering how much his older brother had shared through the messenger. "Don't we all?"

He chuckled and slapped Simon's back. "Come, let's speak outside." He led the way to an open courtyard, shooing chickens as he walked.

Simon's steps were sluggish. He had traveled a long way, but now that he was in Damascus, the burden weighing on him felt heavier than ever.

"Since you will be harbored under my roof," Ananias folded his hands behind his back and paced, "I think it is fair that I know the events that led you here."

Simon folded his muscular arms across his chest. "I think it better they remain in the past."

Ananias didn't miss a step. "While I am of the mind we should not allow our past to define us, I think it wise we remember well the lessons it teaches us. I presume yours has taught you many."

A truth Simon couldn't deny. "It's a long story."

"And I'm an old man, and not getting any younger."

Simon smiled. "I suppose you have a right to the truth."

CHAPTER 19

Simon started his tale from the day he left the potter's house up to the evening he stabbed Joseph, pouring his soul out to the older man.

"I had stabbed my own brother." Simon's throat trembled with the recollection. "Pierced his flesh to teach him a lesson." He lifted the curved blade from his belt and held it up. "I've cleaned it several times, but I know it's still stained with his blood and many others."

"There must be a reason for all this disdain." Ananias kept his eyes on Simon. "You did not come from your mother's womb with such hate."

"No." Simon clenched his jaw. "My hate was forged in the fire of Rome's torment."

"What did Rome do to you that has led you to such a zealous loathing that you would spill blood?"

"They would and have done the same to us given the opportunity. They've spilled so much of our people's blood."

"Is this because of what they did to Jesus?"

The mention of his brother's name brought a tide of emotion; sorrow, pain, and ache. "It's because of what he let happen to me."

"Jesus?" Ananias gave a slight shake of his head. "What did he do?"

Memories Simon had shoved down deep came boiling to the surface. Even as much as he believed Jesus had returned from death as Messiah, Simon still wrestled with many events from his past. Tears burned his eyes. "I was twelve. It should have been the greatest celebration of my life. Jesus was taking me to Jerusalem to be presented to the priests as a man."

"Where was your father?"

"He'd already died in a quarry accident." Simon wiped at his face. "So, the lot fell to my oldest brother to see to the spiritual and physical wellbeing of our entire family." His gaze traveled away. "Jesus left the others in Nazareth so they could keep working. It was just me and him on the trip."

He smiled. "It was a great trip. We talked, and he told me stories about our father as we traveled. It was the most time I had spent alone with my brother."

Simon patted the hilt of his blade. "When we made it near Jerusalem, we stayed with friends in Bethany. Lazarus and his sisters were so excited to see us. I felt like I was stepping into this whole new life that I'd only witnessed from the outside. I was going to be seen as a man and that meant I had to be taken seriously."

He glanced at Ananias. "Jesus took me to the Temple, offered the appropriate sacrifices, and the priest told me I was a man."

"And?"

"And I should have gone back to Lazarus' house." Simon ran a shaking hand through his hair. "But I wanted to celebrate. I was a man. I wanted to enjoy the freedoms of one. So, when Jesus denied me the opportunity, I ran. Jerusalem is a very easy place to hide."

"An easy place for a boy of twelve to get lost in."

"I eventually did. I'd been to the city several times, but always with family. I thought I knew everything." He shrugged. "On my own, I got turned around. I ended up running into some Roman guards. Instead of offering me aid, they demanded I bow down and clean their feet."

"I told them I bowed to Adonai alone, and that I was a man." He lifted his chin. "They found my pride amusing. They took me to an inn and tied me to a pole, forcing drink down my throat and torturing me when I spit it out. They struck me, mocked me, and ripped at my tunic. My humiliation went on for hours."

"And your brother?"

He lowered his head. "When Jesus finally walked through the door of that inn, he hurried over to me and untied my bonds. He slipped off his outer cloak and wrapped it around me. He spoke no words as he helped me."

"Before we reached the door, the Romans tried to stop us. They told Jesus I wasn't done showing them I was a man." Simon's mouth soured with the bile that rose in the back of his throat. "My brother was supposed to be Adonai's Anointed One. He should have avenged me, shown those Romans some real might. But he didn't."

He swallowed hard. "Jesus apologized on my behalf and asked them for forgiveness. I had done nothing wrong." He punched his fist into his palm. "I don't know if they were too drunk or had finally lost interest because they let us pass. Jesus helped me back to Bethany. He spent the whole time telling me how foolish I was for running from him and how much danger I had put myself in."

Fresh tears stung his eyes. "I hated him. I begged him to return to the inn and help me reclaim my honor. But he told me I was the one who needed to beg Adonai for forgiveness."

Simon refused to release more tears. "I saw that day what Adonai's Messiah was all about. He hadn't come to dismantle Rome as we all hoped; he offered only forgiveness and love. Two things one doesn't find on the battlefield."

"Jesus didn't come to start a war."

"That's the worst of it all." Simon returned his dagger to its sheath. "If Jesus was truly Adonai in flesh, as he claimed, then he knew exactly where I was the whole time those Romans were torturing me." He folded his arms. "Jesus could have stopped them long before they bound my hands and spit in my face. He let me suffer.

"When Jesus died, I knew everything I needed to know about my Messiah brother. He was weak. He was a coward. I'd reviled Rome before, but after that day, I purposed to find a way to take down as many of them as I could to purchase back my pride and my name. I would not let a bunch of Gentiles soil me and my people. If our Messiah would not stand up for even the lowest of His people, then we were going to have to stand up for ourselves."

"That's why you left after his death."

Simon nodded. "What good was a dead Messiah going to be to anyone? I knew I had to find others like me. I'd heard stories. I knew Barabbas' name and what he'd done for our people. I wanted to be part of that."

"Did you find what you were looking for with him?"

Simon bit on his lip. "What I learned from my time as a zealot cost me more than I ever wanted to pay. Yet, I was also convinced that if I tried to go back to my old life, I would hang on my own cross for my crimes."

"I'm sure your brother's followers have shared with you what happened to Jesus the day he was arrested."

Simon refused to make eye contact with Ananias.

"How Jesus too had his hands bound, spit on by soldiers, was mocked and beaten." Ananias came close to him. "How he didn't return any of their scorn with hate. How, even dying from wounds and asphyxiation on a cross, he begged Adonai to forgive those who had nailed him there."

"Therein lies the difference between my brother and I." Simon squared his shoulders. "The fire of Rome's persecution revealed my brother's true character. His love and forgiveness won out. When I was put in a similar fire, the dross of my hatred rose to the surface until it blinded me."

A distant creaking brought Simon's hand to his dagger.

Rachel's dark eyes peered around the open doorway. "Forgive me." Her words quaked. "Ima sent for you, Abba."

Simon felt his hand on his dagger and shook out his arm. "It's been a long day." He bowed to Ananias. "Perhaps I should retire for the evening."

"We still have more to discuss."

"Tomorrow," Simon promised. "I need sleep." He hurried past Rachel without looking at her and headed toward the room prepared for him.

CHAPTER 20

The market street was alive around Simon. Sounds of life and business mingled on both sides of the dusty road. He waded through the tide of people like a crocodile in the Nile. His eyes fixed on his target ahead.

Penelope stood alone, admiring the jewelry at a booth. The precious gems in her hand shimmered in the sunlight.

Simon edged closer. His heart beat steadily as he felt the hilt of his dagger with his fingertips.

Penelope lifted a brilliant ruby and held it toward the light. The gemstone caught the sun's rays, sending beams of burgundy around her.

Simon shifted nearer. He released his dagger from its sheath and came upon her. With his blade, he sliced into her midsection and watched the life drain from her eyes.

She reached up with a bloody hand and wiped wet streaks across his face.

When he was certain she had taken her last breath, he withdrew his dagger.

For a split second, her face morphed into Joseph's appearance and back again. The next moment it shifted to Lydia's baby with the unusual eyes.

The hair on the back of Simon's neck stood upright as he watched Penelope's face shift back and forth multiple times until they blended into another face he recognized. Jesus' dark eyes stared at him until the form in front of Simon collapsed.

Simon peered down to see the body, but discovered his hands instead. In one hand, he held his curved dagger. The weapon dripped with fresh blood; the droplets splashed in the sands below. In his other hand, he held a long iron spike. Blood trickled off the end of it and mixed with the blood at his feet, overtaking the blood of Penelope and the others.

Blood drenched his fingertips and soaked into his soul.

He fell to his knees. How could Jesus forgive me?

Simon woke with a jolt. His breath came in short bursts as he attempted to slow his racing heart.

Shadows danced on the wall next to him. He turned toward the doorway and saw Rachel peering at him with an oil lamp next to her face.

"Forgive me," her voice was barely a whisper. "I heard your screams."

Simon ran a shaking hand through his damp hair.

"Who's Penelope?"

He hung his head.

"That was the name you called out."

Simon sucked in a large breath and held on to it while he waited for his heartbeats to slow. When his pulse steadied, he let the air out in a controlled breath.

Rachel sat in the doorway, setting the lamp down, and pulled her knees up to her chest. "I have bad dreams too."

Simon looked at the ceiling. "My father often spoke of his dreams." He gave her a quick glance. "He told us of divine messengers sharing words of peace, comfort, and guidance during the most difficult times of his life."

"That sounds nice." Her lips pulled up into a simple smile that faded quickly. "I wish mine were of peaceful messengers." She dipped her head, keeping her piercing gaze on him from under thick brows and long eyelashes. "It doesn't sound like your dreams are peaceful either."

"No." He shook his head. "My dreams speak nothing of peace. I dream only of death."

"Will you tell me about her?"

Simon lifted a brow.

"Penelope?"

Simon looked at his hands, half expecting to see them dripping with the blood from his dream. They were empty, but shaking. "I know nothing more about her other than her name and that she was a member of a prominent Roman family."

"Then why do you dream of her?"

He kept a firm gaze on Rachel, attempting to measure her reaction to his next words. "Because… I killed her."

Rachel slowly lifted her chin from her knees. "Abba warned me you had done awful things and that I should be careful around you."

"Having a murderer under your roof doesn't bother you?"

"Abba also said you asked for forgiveness."

"Forgiveness doesn't change the past."

"It's not supposed to." Rachel shook her head. "It's supposed to change the guilty."

Simon felt the words echo through him. Something in them rang true, but they also clashed against something else inside he couldn't name.

"Why did you kill her?"

He lifted a shoulder. "I belonged to a group of zealots. I was told she was a mark." He shifted his gaze. "I found out later that the one who paid the price of her death had a different target in mind. It turns out my own sister was seeking to murder the betrothed of the woman. But our leader switched the marks without telling me."

"Why?"

"Politics."

"I mean, why did your sister want the woman's betrothed dead?"

"Saul had killed her betrothed, or at least he'd been instrumental in the murder. My sister was seeking revenge." Simon shook his head. "All it did was provide fodder for the already burning fire of war."

Rachel slowly lowered her chin to her knees. "There's too much war and death in our world."

"Is that what you dream of?"

She closed her eyes. "I dream of pain, screams of agony, of metal bars that slam, and of tears. So many tears."

"And these tears, are they yours?"

Rachel shook her head. "I don't know. The dreams are simply flashes. But the pain stays with me even when I wake."

Simon was all too familiar with the feeling.

"Are you staying?"

Her question seemed to come out of nowhere. "As long as your father allows me."

"My father's a good man."

That much had been evident to Simon. He considered the fact that no one could say as much about him. He lay down and stared at the ceiling. "How long have you had these dreams of tears?"

"A few years. They startled me the first night so bad, I refused to return to sleep." She lifted a shoulder. "They are so frequent now that I don't even bother sharing them with my parents."

Simon turned his attention toward her and watched as she drew in the dust.

"They started the night before my abba shared with us about what happened to your brother." She let her finger graze over the packed earth. "Father told us about the traveling teacher and how much he believed Jesus was the Messiah we've been waiting for."

Her fingers paused. "When he found out one of Jesus' followers had betrayed him and his own people had turned him over to the Romans, he knew all the sayings were true." She lifted her eyes to Simon. "When we heard about Jesus rising from the dead a few days later and the others who crawled out of the tombs on the same day, it was enough to confirm my father's faith in Him."

Simon rolled to his side and lifted himself to his arm. "If you and your family are so certain of my brother's claims, then why are you tortured by such sorrow-filled dreams?"

In the quiet of the next few moments, Simon could feel Rachel withdrawing.

"I believe Jesus is Messiah." She grabbed her oil lamp and rose to her feet. "I'm also wise enough to know that just because Messiah has come doesn't mean the world has been set right. There's still much for Adonai to redeem and restore."

As he listened to her retreating footsteps, he wondered if her words were true. And, if they were, was he included in her assessment of the work still left undone?

CHAPTER 21

Simon woke the next morning to the smell of baking bread. He stirred and rose, but his muscles protested. Sleep had returned to him after his talk with Rachel, but it was too short.

In the main area, the women were already busy with daily preparations.

Rachel gave him a nod of understanding as he moved into the room. She rose from her place and prepared a few simple items that she placed at the edge of the table for him.

He inclined his head to her with thanks and broke his fast, surrounded by the hum of routine.

It wasn't long before Ananias joined him at the table; a look of obvious concern plastered on his face. "Are our accommodations not enough to allow for peaceful nights?"

Simon felt heat crawl up his neck. "I can assure you my torture has nothing to do with your hospitality."

"Well, that certainly is good news."

"I will attempt to quiet my suffering." Simon glanced at Rachel, who turned toward them but didn't add to the conversation. He wondered how she had learned to quiet her nightly sufferings.

The men ate in silence until Ananias rose. "Come, Simon."

Shoving the last bite of bread into his mouth, Simon rose to obey.

Ananias led Simon toward the market. "I thought I'd introduce you to some of the others. Seeing as how you'll be staying here in Damacus for a while."

Simon's insides itched. While he didn't expect to be pampered as a king in Ananias' house, he wasn't sure if becoming involved with the Way Followers in the city would be beneficial for either side.

The older man took his time along the market street, presenting Simon to many of the merchants.

Simon noticed the collection of wares available were much more numerous than many of the other cities he visited due to the city's position on the trade routes. Furs from the north of animals he'd never seen, spices from the east he couldn't name, and fruits from exotic lands were all fully obtainable for any buyers' delight.

Yet, it was the billows of smoke and the smell of fire that drew Simon's attention further. Drawing near, the clamor of hammers on steel echoed around him.

"Ahh." Ananias waved ahead of them. "Simon, I haven't yet introduced you to my sons." He took them closer to the large booth. "This is Caleb and Boaz."

Simon inclined his head toward the brothers. He noted the men shared many features of both each other and their parents.

Caleb hesitated his swing only long enough to nod in Simon's direction.

Boaz approached Simon. "So, this is the trouble maker we've heard so much about?" He pulled his muscular arms together over his chest.

Simon's mouth soured with words he would have easily let slip in his former days. He elected instead to let his gaze drop to the display of steel before him. The striking assortment of blades glinted in the bright sunlight. His fingers danced over the unusual patterns in the metal. They appeared as churned waves or cut wood.

"Damascus steel." Boaz lifted one of the blades and rubbed his calloused thumb down the side. "There's nothing else like it."

Simon selected a short blade. It was wonderfully balanced. He ran his finger along the edge and pressed on the blade. The metal was hard but also flexible and the edge was incredibly sharp.

"I see you've got an eye for metal."

Setting the Damascus dagger down, Simon retrieved his curved blade from under the folds of his tunic.

Boaz's eyes flashed.

Simon eased the weapon from its sheath.

"May I?"

Flipping the dagger's end, Simon held the handle toward Boaz.

He gripped the handle and held it up. "An impressive weapon to be sure." Boaz hummed to himself, carefully inspecting the dagger. "But it is in desperate need of cleaning and a good sharpening."

Simon's gut twisted. He was the only one with full knowledge of the stains the weapon held and why the blade lacked its edge.

Boaz smiled. "It would be a pleasure to restore it to its former glory."

Relinquishing the sheath, Simon nodded his agreement. Nothing would ever remove the stains of the past, but he would not condemn a good blade to rot simply because of his mistakes. His attention returned to the Damascus dagger. "Perhaps I shall earn enough to purchase one of these."

"My good man." Boaz huffed as he returned Simon's dagger to its sheath. "One does not merely purchase a Damascus blade, but the years of experience of the blade maker."

The edges of Simon's mouth twitched. Something in Boaz's voice reminded him of Rachel. "Truly?"

Boaz leaned over and retrieved the dagger in front of Simon. "Take this piece here." He held it up. "Look at these incredible lines that have been achieved through endless toil of fold after fold of the steel."

As if rehearsed, Caleb slammed his hammer down on the blade he was fashioning.

The sound bounced through Simon.

"Months." Boaz clicked his tongue. "Months of sweat and blood go into each of these blades."

Caleb struck again.

"Why, these are not mere blades." Boaz lifted the dagger so the light caught it just right. "These are works of art imbued with the knowledge of generations of craftsmen."

"Save your speeches for a buyer with a full coin purse." Simon held up his hands. "Mine is empty."

Ananias came forward with a bolstered chuckle. "That's enough boys." He slapped Simon on the back. "I've got more people to introduce Simon to."

"I'll take care of this." Boaz raised Simon's dagger. "No need to worry."

Simon gave both men a nod of departure and continued on with Ananias. Making his way along the street, he noticed his uneven steps. The weight of the dagger that never left his side was replaced by a strange emptiness.

"Simon, I'd like you to meet a dear friend of mine."

Ananias' introduction and wave toward a man heading their direction turned Simon's attention away from his belt.

"This is Joseph of Cyprus."

Simon greeted the man with a bow.

"Barnabas," the man corrected.

"Forgive me. I forgot." Ananias held his head. "Barnabas, this is another of James' brothers."

"I've heard much about you." Barnabas bowed his head to Simon. "I met your siblings in Jerusalem, and they spoke of you."

Simon lifted a curious brow. He wondered which side of his story his brothers had shared with this man.

"Ah." Barnabas reached toward his belt. "I nearly forgot. This is for you, Ananias." He produced a money pouch and handed it to the older man. "Along with the prayers of many of our brothers and sisters."

"Thank you, friend." Ananias accepted the pouch and tucked it into his belt. "We have many in need that these funds will bless, along with the equal sacrifice of prayers." He clapped his hands. "Do you have time to share a report?"

"I do."

"Well, then walk with us." Ananias set the pace.

Simon listened as the man from Cyprus shared about his most recent travels and updated Ananias on the progress of spreading Jesus' teachings through the regions.

He wrestled with the peculiar idea of strangers sharing stories and teachings of his brother. It didn't seem that long ago that Jesus was a simple craftsman providing for his simple family. Now, his name struck fear into the minds of the reigning authorities and hope into the souls of the people. Could Simon find the courage to share as freely as Barnabas when a great debt of sin clung to his name?

"Thank you." Ananias stopped at the end of the market. "It has been quite encouraging to hear of the growing support for Way Followers. Will you be staying to share this news with the others?"

"I'm afraid I can't stay." Barnabas shook his head. "I will be returning to Jerusalem soon. I have family there that I long to see." He turned to Simon. "And I'm looking forward to visiting with your family too." He smiled. "Shall I pass along a message?"

Simon flicked his gaze to Ananias. "Tell them I'm well." He turned back to Barnabas. "I have found a safe harbor and plan to make repairs to my battered ship."

Barnabas lifted a brow. "You sailed here?"

Ananias let out a booming laugh. "No, my friend, I will explain it to you." He wrapped an arm around Barnabas' neck.

For a moment, something lifted off Simon's shoulders. His burdens were many and his fears were real, but listening to the news of Jesus' message spreading wide and sharing the laughter of a jest gave a glimmer of hope. If he could hold onto the flicker, he just might be able to survive whatever lay ahead.

CHAPTER 22

Another sleepless night caused Simon to be awake with the rising sun. Fortunately for him, it seemed every member of Ananias' household woke by first light. Sounds of daily preparations and breaking fasts stirred him from the borrowed room.

Simon collected his morning's portion from Rachel. The dark places under her eyes told him she probably rested as well as he had. If only he could trade his few hours of sleep to give her a full night of peace.

Caleb and Boaz finished their meals quickly and headed out for their day's labor.

Envy crawled in Simon's soul. How much easier life is for a man when he need only worry about setting his hands to work. Boaz had been true to his word to restore Simon's curved blade which now hung in its proper place inside his tunic.

Ananias joined Simon at the table and shared of the plans for the day.

Simon had agreed to meet more followers in the hopes of finding a place among them to earn his hiding place.

The older man rose. "We shall head out—" Ananias' words twisted into a scream of agony.

Simon watched Ananias fold forward in an unnatural way and slam his knees on the ground. His hands came up to his ears as he cried out.

"Abba!" Rachel and the other two girls rushed to his side. "What is it?"

"Here I am, Lord." Ananias lifted his eyes toward the ceiling.

Simon jumped to his feet and looked up, but saw nothing.

Mariah kneeled beside her husband. "Ananias?"

"Here I am, Lord!"

Simon watched Ananias' face drain of color and his eyes focused on something beyond his natural sight.

"Lord," Ananias lifted his hands, "I have heard from many about this man, how much evil he has done to your saints at Jerusalem. And now he has authority from the chief priests to bind all who call on your name."

Rachel's head came up in a quick movement.

Simon locked eyes with her.

Ananias said nothing more for a few moments longer and then he collapsed onto the ground.

"Ananias!" Mariah shrieked.

Simon shook the older man until he sat up.

Ananias looked around. "I've got to go." He attempted to rise on shaky legs.

Mariah grabbed her husband's arm. "I'm going to get a physician. You just collapsed."

"Didn't you hear the voice?" Ananias searched their faces. "I've got to leave at once."

"We heard nothing, Abba." Rachel grabbed his arm. "What did you hear?"

"Adonai." He stood and reached out to steady himself on the edge of the table.

Rachel held onto her father's other arm. "What did the Lord say?"

Ananias looked at Simon. "You heard nothing?"

Simon shook his head. "Only your words."

"It was Adonai. Speaking as clearly as I hear every one of you right now." He kept his gaze on Simon. "He said, 'Rise and go to the street called Straight, and at the house of Judas look for a man of Tarsus named Saul, for behold, he is praying, and he has seen in a vision a man named Ananias come in and lay his hands on him so that he might regain his sight.'"

Simon's heart quickened. "Saul? Saul's here? In Damascus?" The shields of his assumed protection cracked.

"When I argued, the Lord said, 'Go, for he is a chosen instrument of mine to carry My name before the Gentiles and kings and the children of Israel. For I will show him how much he must suffer for the sake of My name.'" Ananias shook his head. "I've got to go."

"You can't." Simon stood in his way. "This is Saul we're talking about."

"Adonai has ordered. I must obey."

"You'd be walking into a trap."

"Simon," Ananias gripped Simon's shoulder, "I will allow no one to stand in the way of my obedience to Adonai."

"You're willing to risk not only your safety but your family's as well?" He waved toward the group of women surrounding them.

Ananias gazed at each face before returning his attention to Simon. "If Adonai has given instructions, He will be the one to guide my steps." He pushed past Simon and headed toward the door.

"Simon, you can't let Abba do this." Rachel twisted a cloth in her hand. "Go with him."

He looked into her bright eyes, filling with unshed tears. "If I go, Saul will recognize me. I'd be in chains before I was able to get both feet in the door."

"Please? You must keep my father safe."

Simon grunted and stormed out of the house after Ananias. He caught up with him as the older man turned toward Straight Street. "Ananias, return to your home. I beg you. Don't show your face to Saul. He's here to hunt Way Followers. He's here hunting me."

Ananias continued his focused march down the road.

"How did they even let him into the city?" Simon kept up with the man's quick pace. "He should not be in the land occupied by Syria."

Ananias didn't slow his pace. "Adonai mentioned this man is from Tarsus. Is that correct?"

"Yes, that's true."

"Rome controls Tarsus." Ananias' explanation was provided as simply as if he were speaking of the weather.

"You're referring to Saul's Roman citizenship?"

"Roman status opens paths we can only dream of." Ananias searched the fronts of houses. "He could travel almost anywhere without question."

"What would give him the right to hunt outside Jerusalem?"

Ananias hesitated. "The High Priest has given him letters to arrest anyone he wants."

"How do you know that?"

"Adonai revealed it to me." He hurried on.

Simon scurried after him. "If that's true, we must leave Damascus. It's no longer safe here for us."

Ananias paused at a tall building and stared up at it. "I appreciate your concern, but I must obey." He stepped toward the open doorway. "Greetings to the owner of this house."

Glancing around, Simon searched for any answer to the madness in which he found himself entangled.

A man appeared in the archway.

Ananias stepped to the man. "Are you Judas?"

"I am."

"Are you giving lodging to a man called Saul from Tarsus?"

"I am." Judas looked at the two of them. "Who are you?"

"Ananias."

"Ananias?" Judas lifted a shaking hand and waved them in. "Come inside. He said you'd come. He's been waiting for you."

Ananias ducked into the darkness.

Simon grunted. He looked around once more, but finding no other solution, he followed Ananias inside.

Judas led them through the house to a back room where two temple guards stood in front of a door.

Simon took note of the two. One appeared much older, with skin darkened by days in the sun. The other was not that much younger, but his thin beard revealed he still had many more days ahead of him.

Flashes spread across Simon's mind; the younger guard reminded him too much of Ursus. Splashes of red filled his vision, and he fought to maintain focus. "Sanhedrin guards," he whispered to Ananias as they approached. He eyed the broad swords at their sides. "We'll be behind iron bars for sure."

"Trust Adonai," Ananias whispered back. "It's all any of us can do." He stepped toward the two soldiers. "My name is Ananias. I am here to see Saul of Tarsus."

The younger guard looked at the older one. "He said a man named Ananias would come."

"It's been three days." The darker-skinned guard appraised both men with a long stare. "State your business."

"I come in the name of Adonai." Ananias stepped forward. "He has ordered me to pray over Saul to heal him of his affliction."

The older guard hung his head. "Saul has not eaten or taken a drink in the three days we've been in Damascus. I fear if he does not take something soon, he will perish."

"Why do you care for such a man?" Simon growled.

He set a firm glare on Simon. "I'm responsible for his well-being. If I return a dead Pharisee to the council, they will gladly add two more to the total without hesitation."

Ananias raised his hand to call for peace. "What happened to Saul?"

"We don't know." The younger lifted his shoulder. "As we came near the city, some vision knocked Saul to the ground. We saw nothing; though we thought we heard…" He glanced at his companion.

The older shook his head as if denying their shared experience.

"When we got him off the ground," the younger continued, "he had lost his sight. We brought him here, but he has grown worse since we arrived."

"Allow us to pass." Ananias squared his shoulders. "This is the will of Adonai."

The guards shared a concerned look.

"Do as he says." Simon stepped aside. "Or face a power greater than the council."

CHAPTER 23

Reluctantly, the guards stepped aside.

Simon waved Ananias ahead of himself, allowing the older man to enter first. Once inside, Simon searched the room and found Saul curled up on a mat against the wall.

Saul startled at the sound of their approach. "Who's there?"

Ananias moved toward Saul with outstretched arms. "I am Ananias."

"Ananias?" Saul rose to his feet, tripping among the goat skin blankets. "Adonai said you'd come."

Simon kept a skeptical glare on Saul. The man's eyes seemed to be fixed on a distant space. He was far from the predator Simon left in Jerusalem. Adonai had reduced him to a blind and faltering fool. His skin was pale from lack of nourishment. It was a pathetic sight to see a powerful man lowered to such depths. Simon almost felt sorry for him... almost.

Ananias moved closer and laid his hands on Saul's face. "Brother Saul, the Lord Jesus who appeared to you on the road has sent me so that you may regain your sight and be filled with the Holy Spirit."

Saul closed his eyes and leaned into Ananias' touch.

When Ananias removed his hands, Simon saw something fall off Saul's face. His skin crawled at the sight. "What was that?" He pointed to the scale-like objects falling to the ground and dissolving in the dust.

"I can see." Saul slowly lowered his gaze toward Ananias. "Praise Adonai. He has restored my vision!"

The two guards stormed into the room.

"I can see!" Saul shouted again, leaping toward the armored men. "I can see!"

Simon put his hand on his dagger. This could have been a clever ruse to get them in the same room.

Saul came closer, shouting with joy.

Nearing the crazed man, Simon saw something flash in Saul's eyes that made him drop his hand. The same fire he'd seen in Martha's eyes was there in Saul's. It was an unusual sign that Simon didn't understand.

Jumping from spot to spot, Saul shouted, "Food! Bring me food."

Ananias looked at the two soldiers. "You heard the man."

They both disappeared through the doorway.

Simon moved toward Ananias. "You've completed your assignment. We should leave now."

"Not yet." Ananias went to Saul. "Brother Saul, please tell us what happened to you on the road."

Saul paced around the room, twisting his hands and wiping at his face. "I was on my way here with papers from the High Priest. I'd finally convinced them to let me come to the synagogues here in

Damascus to interrogate and arrest Way Followers." He shook his finger. "I knew many were hiding here." He stopped mid-stride. "You," he pointed to Simon, "I was hunting you and the others."

Simon's fingers ached to reach for his blade.

Saul waved his hand around. "As we were drawing near to the city, I saw a light from heaven all around us." He picked up his pacing. "I was on the ground before I knew it and I heard a voice call my name, 'Saul, Saul, why are you persecuting Me?'"

He continued in a circle. "I didn't recognize the voice, but I recognized the authority it carried, so I asked him to identify himself. He said, 'I am Jesus, whom you are persecuting. But rise and enter the city, and you will be told what you are to do.' The guards who accompanied me said they heard the voice too, but didn't see who was speaking. When the voice stopped speaking and the light disappeared, I realized I had lost my sight."

Saul touched under his eyes. "The guards led me by the hand inside the city and here to Judas' house." He stopped in front of Ananias. "I've been fasting and praying for three days. Jesus informed me that a man named Ananias would arrive and lay hands on me, resulting in the restoration of my sight."

The older guard entered with a loaf of bread and handed it to Saul. "There's more coming."

Tearing at the offering, Saul lifted a piece to his lips but hesitated. He lowered the bite. "I need to be baptized." He looked at Ananias. "Is there water nearby?"

"The Abana River cuts through part of the city." Ananias moved toward the door. "I can take you there and baptize you myself."

Saul handed the loaf back to the guard and followed Ananias out of the room.

Simon gave a quick glance to the guard and hurried after them. "Wait." He caught up to them. "What are you doing?"

"I must be baptized." Saul pointed forward. "As John ben Zechariah did to those who were preparing their hearts for Messiah."

"Why now?" Simon hurried to keep up with them. "Shouldn't we talk about what happened?"

Ananias chuckled. "Forgive the boy. He's still learning to see with more than his eyes."

The three men rushed through the city toward the river.

Ananias showed Saul where they could descend.

Simon followed, keeping his eyes on Ananias. He didn't know Saul's motive for coming to the water, but he would not allow Ananias out of his sight. He would return Rachel's father to her in the same condition as when they departed.

Ananias and Saul waded out into the water until the stream came to their waists.

Simon went in only a few steps.

"Saul," Ananias lifted one hand toward the sky, "my brother, I baptize you in the name of Jesus of Nazareth." He carefully lowered Saul into the water and raised him up again.

When Saul broke the surface, he shouted praises.

Ananias joined him with even louder shouts.

The two sloshed back toward the shore.

"There." Simon waved toward the stream. "You've been baptized. Our dealings with you are finished. Be on your way."

Saul ran a hand through his wet hair to express the water. "I must return to Judas' home and speak to the guards. I need to send them back to the council with news of what has happened to me."

The two men dripped with water as they marched through the city.

Simon kept his distance. Saul's claims and his display of conversion had not convinced him.

Ananias and Saul spoke in excited tones while they walked back toward Judas' house. They parted ways at the door, and Ananias returned to Simon's side.

The walk back to Ananias' home was tense.

Simon's disgust was difficult to hide.

"You're free to speak your mind with me." Ananias hesitated at the end of Straight Street.

"I can't believe you trust that beast."

"You witnessed his eyes opening. You heard his story."

"A story too perfect to believe." Simon spat. "He comes here claiming to be one of us as a ruse to hunt more of us." His hands turned to fists. "You heard him admit that he's still in possession of papers which give him the legal right to arrest men and women who follow the Way."

"Simon, you're so bitter and full of anger that you are blind yourself."

Simon's chest tightened.

"Adonai has done a great miracle before your own eyes and you still hold Saul's past actions against him."

"He's a vengeful Pharisee seeking to lock me away and all those who follow my brother."

Ananias shook his head. "If you always look at Saul's past, you will never see what Adonai is doing with him right now." He picked up his pace toward his own home. "In my vision, Adonai told me Saul is His chosen instrument to carry Adonai's name to the Gentiles. But I also saw that Adonai will allow much suffering in Saul's life for His name's sake."

"Saul is the one who has caused much suffering."

"And he will live a life full of suffering." Ananias groaned. "But his life will also be a testament to Adonai's glory." He paused at the entrance to his house and turned to Simon. "Based on James' testimony of your changed life, I've provided refuge for you and believed your repentance from your former life without question."

Simon's neck burned.

"In many ways, you and Saul are on similar paths. Adonai has great plans for both of you. How would you feel if you discovered my unforgiveness when you arrived here?" He stepped just inside the doorway. "The question is, now that Saul has accepted your brother's forgiveness, what are you going to offer him?" He turned and walked inside.

Simon stood outside, contemplating the older man's words. He had been quick to demand others to look beyond his past while he still held Saul's against him. He was not yet ready to forget all of Saul's charges. He would at least attempt to see if Saul's conversion was real before he called him brother.

CHAPTER 24

A few days later, Simon accompanied Ananias to one of the local synagogues. The older man had convinced the Rabbi there to allow Saul to speak and convinced Simon to be in attendance. Two seemingly impossible tasks in Simon's estimation.

Inside the simple building, Simon searched the faces of those present. A handful of men sat on one side of the square room. Typically, the area would be filled with men, women, and children to hear their Rabbi or a guest speaker. It seemed the faith community still held their doubts concerning the rumors circulating about Saul's miraculous conversion.

Simon settled on a low step near the doorway. He wanted to have easy access to flee in case Saul planned to use the arrest papers still in his possession. The same man who'd been invited to speak to the gathering and been arresting believers only days ago, now claimed to be one of them.

When Saul entered the room, Simon fixed a skeptical gaze on him. The man, whose very name struck fear into the hearts of Way Followers, seemed to shrink before Simon's eyes. Gone was the puffed-up predator. Today, Saul was timid, slow, and almost meek in his appearance and stature. His eyes, still boiling with zeal, seemed to be the only remnant of his former self and even they appeared to have been dipped into a silversmith's fire.

After the traditional prayers, songs, and readings, Saul was permitted to ascend the platform and took his seat on the bema. He fumbled over his first few words, clearing his throat multiple times and keeping his gaze on the ground.

As his voice gained strength and conviction, something stirred inside Simon.

Saul spoke of his encounter with the risen Jesus, of the blinding light that knocked him to the ground, and of the powerful voice that called his name and offered him a message of redemption and salvation. "It is this same message I bring to you today." He glanced around the room.

Despite the power and passion of Saul's words, Simon remained suspicious. How could he trust a man who had once been a persecutor of the very faith he now held? How could he believe the words of someone who only days before sought to destroy everything he held dear?

Simon heard sincerity in Saul's words, a fervor that spoke of a genuine transformation wrought by an encounter with the divine. Try as he might to resist, Simon found himself drawn in by the pull of Saul's appeal, his doubts giving way to a glimmer of hope.

Could it really be true that an encounter with Jesus had changed Saul from oppressor to believer?

As Saul spoke, the seeds of doubt in Simon's mind and soul were plucked out one by one.

Reaching the last point of his testimony, Saul stood and spread his arms toward the meager crowd. "Jesus is the Son of God."

The men murmured to each other.

One of them rose to his feet. "Is not this the man who made havoc in Jerusalem of those who called upon this name?"

Another added to the speculation. "Has he not come here to bring them bound before the chief priests?"

Among the other verbal accusations flung in Saul's direction, the synagogue's Rabbi moved forward to end the meeting before tempers rose to unmanageable heights.

The men asked no questions of Saul and left, still clamoring to one another about the message they had heard him share.

As the congregation dispersed, Simon lingered in the shadows of the synagogue, his thoughts swirling. Amid the turmoil of his inner conflict, a voice whispered in the depths of his soul.

Love your enemies and pray for those who persecute you, so that you may be sons of your Father who is in heaven.

He recognized the calming voice of his brother and stepped forward to confront Saul.

Saul sat with his head bowed low. He slowly raised his head to meet Simon's gaze and squinted for a few moments until realization dawned on his face. "You came to Judas' house the other day with Ananias." His gaze shifted momentarily to the older man before returning his attention to Simon. "But I remember you from that day in the market…"

Simon heard the crack in the man's tone.

"Penelope."

The name hit Simon in the gut and twisted like a blade.

"You're the one who killed my betrothed."

Simon's blood ran cold. His mind spun with the implications of Saul's words. They were true; there was no hiding from them. "My zeal blinded me. I believed what I was doing was Adonai's will to dismantle the oppression of Rome against our people."

Saul closed his eyes. "Oh, how very similar we are." He opened his eyes. "You see, my zeal also blinded me. I believed I was also doing Adonai's will by persecuting those who followed the teachings of Jesus. In my quest to dismantle what I saw as heresy; I lost sight of the truth."

Simon's chest grew heavy with understanding for his former enemy.

"My pride blinded me." Saul shook his head. "Jesus had every right to take away my sight. I certainly didn't deserve to have it restored."

"I could not see the truth of my brother's teaching until it was too late."

"Your brother?" Saul squinted. "You're one of His siblings?"

Simon nodded. "The man named Stephen that you approved to have stoned; he was also my sister's betrothed."

Saul rose from the bema seat and took a step forward. "Stephen." He put a hand on his chest. "May Adonai have mercy on my soul. Is that why you killed Penelope?"

Simon lowered his gaze. "I knew nothing of your betrothed. It was Barabbas who switched the targets on me. The original buyer hired us to murder you, not the woman." He raised his gaze. "I didn't know it was supposed to be you and I didn't know it was my own sister's revenge for the murder of Stephen."

"Someone hired you to kill me?" Saul held his head. "And by Adonai's hand, you killed Penelope instead. May Adonai have mercy on all our souls."

"I don't deserve forgiveness." Simon swallowed hard. "But I feel I must ask it of you."

Saul reached out to clasp Simon's shoulder. "We've all made poor choices. We all need forgiveness. Fortunately for us, Jesus is offering just that. Neither of us can allow these choices to define us.

Instead, we must both choose the path of repentance and redemption, of love and forgiveness. I chose it, Simon. What will you choose?"

Simon nodded. "I choose forgiveness."

Saul pulled him in for an embrace.

In the arms of his former enemy, Simon knew Saul's transformation was genuine. The man had truly witnessed the power of Adonai's grace to heal even the deepest wounds of the soul. In that realization, he found hope for himself and his future and a renewed sense of purpose in his own journey of faith.

Separating from the embrace, Simon looked into the burning gaze of Saul. There he discovered a fellow traveler on the road to redemption, a newfound friend, and a brother in Christ.

"I have good news." Ananias approached them. "The Rabbi has agreed to allow you to speak again, Saul. There are many more who need to hear your message."

For several weeks, Simon sat in attendance as Saul shared about Jesus with anyone who visited the synagogue. Word spread like fire through the city about the hunter-turned-convert. Several other Rabbis invited Saul to speak in their synagogues. Through Saul's testimony, many heard of Jesus and joined the Way.

Seeing Adonai at work, Simon decided to remain in Damascus. The city he once hoped would be his place of refuge became his place of redemption. He settled into service alongside Ananias and others.

After months of speeches in synagogues, Saul expanded his visits to the surrounding areas. Eventually spending less and less time in the city and more and more time away.

Simon prayed for his brother and companion in the faith and waited with hope for the day they would reunite.

CHAPTER 25

A.D. 38, Damascus

The sun lifted in the sky as Simon made his way through the bustling streets of Damascus, his heart pounding with anticipation. The city had become as familiar to him as Nazareth and Jerusalem; in three years it had become home.

For nearly two years, he awaited Saul's return from the deserts of Arabia. He received word that the traveling teacher was returning to Damascus and was eager to visit with the community of believers who had first welcomed him after his conversion.

Simon approached the city gates. The teeth of iron no longer held a fearful grip on him. Even the guards who patrolled the area had become brothers. He dipped his head toward Jamal. "Shalom."

"Salaam." The Syrian guard greeted him with a warm embrace. "What brings you to the gates so early?"

"Saul's expected to return today."

"Truly?" Jamal's eyebrows jumped.

"I have the task of escorting him to Ananias' house. We're preparing a feast to welcome him."

Jamal's smile widened. "I'm looking forward to hearing him teach again."

"As are we all. I'm sure he has many stories to share from his travels."

Simon settled himself outside the gate, keeping his gaze on the horizon to see the first sign of Saul. While waiting, he rummaged through his memories of the last two years of his friend's absence. He was sure they both would have much to share with one another.

It wasn't long before Simon noticed a familiar form cresting the distant line between earth and sky. He rose, eager to embrace his returning brother.

With warmth and affection that found its source in the soul, the two embraced one another in a bond of brotherhood that transcended words.

Saul was the first to find his voice. "It's good to see you, my friend."

"We have missed your presence dearly." Simon couldn't control the emotions choking his words. His heart overflowed with gratitude and joy.

"Come then." Saul stepped toward the gate. "We shall not keep the rest waiting. I'm eager to share about what Adonai has been doing among the Gentiles."

The two chatted on easier topics as they made their way through Damascus toward the home of Ananias.

"There's a large crowd waiting for you." Simon hurried his steps. "And even more who've promised to hear you speak in the synagogues."

"I'm looking forward to it."

Approaching the house, Simon's heart squeezed. Standing in the doorway, with a radiant smile, was Rachel. Her eyes sparkled with joy and expectation. "Better go ahead," he whispered to Saul. "I've got to answer for my early departure."

Saul hummed with understanding.

"Shalom, Rachel." Saul kissed both of her cheeks. "I'm glad to see you are well."

"We've been eagerly awaiting your arrival." She returned the affection. "Abba's waiting inside."

Saul nodded and entered the house.

Simon waited for Rachel to turn her brilliant gaze on him. Her dark eyes shone like the sun breaking through dark clouds.

"You didn't tell me you were leaving so early." Her smile fell on one side. "I wanted to accompany you this morning."

"I know." He took a cautious step toward her. "I didn't want to disturb your slumber."

"It should be my decision what disturbs my slumber." She folded her arms over her chest.

He couldn't help the smile that tugged at the corners of his lips. The woman who had captured his heart and become his beloved wife in the time since Saul's departure glowed with life that caused her midsection to protrude against her tunic. She was radiant, even in her attempts to feign anger. "Forgive me." He pecked her cheek with a soft kiss. "I knew once Saul returned to our fold, I wouldn't get a moment alone with him. Forgive a selfish man who desired but a few moments with my friend before his attention was seized by everyone in Damascus."

Rachel sighed. "I suppose I can forgive you this one offense." She held up a finger. "But no more."

He kissed her finger and ducked inside.

The air in Ananias' house was alive with the sounds of laughter and conversation. People passed Saul from person to person, with everyone attempting to speak over everyone else.

"Friends," Anania's voice boomed over the chaos. "I'm sure our guest will be happy to visit with each of you but allow him space to breathe. We would not seek to crush our dear brother with the weight of our love."

The group of believers spent the day hearing story after story from Saul and feasting his return.

Simon looked around at the faces of his fellow believers while a sense of belonging washed over him. With Saul back among them, it seemed everything was as it should be once more.

As the day wore into evening, several people retired to their own homes, leaving behind promises of their return.

Simon sat between Saul and Ananias, their voices mingling in a chorus of laughter and conversation.

While the others of the house prepared for sleep, the three men remained.

When the first quiet moment passed over them since Saul entered the house, Ananias broke it with concern. "Saul, I've been praying for your return, but I worry for you."

Saul took a long draw from his stone cup. "Oh?"

"You know I'm well respected in the city." Ananias glared at him. "I keep an ear on all the news related to Damascus to keep our population of believers safe."

"And your efforts are greatly appreciated."

"Before your return, I've heard many rumors."

Simon perked up. This was the first he had heard of his father-in-law's distress over Saul's return to Damascus.

"Brother Saul," Ananias hesitated, "since the death of Tiberius Caesar, Gaius Caligula has risen to emperor."

"I'm aware." Saul's words held an indifferent tone.

"Then you know of the changes he's made concerning imperial policies." Ananias's silver brow lifted with certainty. "How he's given various regions to his allies, including handing Damascus over to the Nabataean king, Aretas, because of the king's previous support to Gaius' father."

Simon's attempts to remain out of the politics of Damascus failed as this news now stirred concern in his soul. "This King Aretas is the same whose daughter was married and divorced from Herod Antipas, who then married his stepbrother's wife, Herodias." Simon looked at Saul. "It was opposition to that unholy union that led to the beheading of my cousin, John."

Saul looked between both men. "What does this have to do with me?"

Ananias reached for Saul. "There was a reason Aretas wanted Damascus back under Nabataean control. He's trying to stop the conversion of Nabateans to the Way. The very mission our Lord has given you." He gave a quick glance to Simon. "With pressure from King Aretas, the governor has issued warnings and made it legal to arrest any who try to convert citizens to become followers of Jesus."

Simon's chest tightened. Peace had reigned over him for two years and with one piece of news, his entire wall of contentment crumbled. If Aretas didn't want Syrians to become Way Followers, to what lengths would he go to prevent it from happening?

"I fear for you." Ananias patted Saul's hand. "Adonai has shown me many things. News of much more has reached my ears."

Simon recalled his father-in-law's constant prayers for Saul. Ever since Ananias' vision to go to Saul and be the instrument used to restore his sight, the proud man had humbled himself in prayer with the weight of Saul's future sufferings. Simon had added many of his own petitions since that day.

CHAPTER 26

Only weeks after Simon's joyful reunion with Saul, word reached Ananias of a plot against Saul.

The three men gathered for prayer.

After pleas to Adonai, Simon turned his petitions to Ananias. "Where can we send him?"

The older man pulled at his long beard. "Further north?"

"Into the king's hands, I think not."

"I know where I must go." Saul rose with his body as calm as his voice.

Simon wondered how he kept his composure under such pressure. "Where?"

"Jerusalem."

"No." Simon dismissed the idea at once. "The followers won't accept you there. They won't believe you've changed."

"I must." He put a hand on Simon's arm. "There are wrongs there I must make right."

"I don't understand."

Saul took in a breath. "Before I left Jerusalem, I imprisoned many Way Followers." He let out his breath slowly and controlled. "When I first came here to Damascus, I was so overwhelmed with everything that happened I had forgotten my past in Jerusalem. But I must return."

"What is so important there that you would risk your life? If the Jews and the authorities here have combined forces to kill you, the ones in Jerusalem are sure to still be hungry for your blood."

"Simon," he squeezed his arm, "your youngest sister was one of the ones I put in chains."

Simon shook off his friend's grip. "What?"

"She, along with many others, sit in chains because of me."

"She must be so frightened." Simon rose to his feet. "Let me be the one to go to her."

"If you return to that city, they'll put you in a matching pair of shackles." Ananias slowly made his way to stand. "Remember, to Rome, you're still a zealot. Unlike Adonai, they don't take conversion as payment for past crimes."

"I have to see her. I can't stay here while my sister rots in a dirty cell." Simon collapsed in defeat. "I'm responsible for her."

"Even in Sheol, Adonai will be with her." Ananias put his hand on Simon's shoulder. "You can't go to Jerusalem. Rachel needs you here. Your child come any day."

"Rachel." Simon's wife sprang to his thoughts. "She would never forgive me if I left now." He looked up at Saul. "Do you truly believe you can free Salome?"

"I can go before the council." Saul spread his hands wide. "I can plead her case and try to get the charges against her dropped."

Ananias turned to Saul. "That will be a difficult enough task for you. But how are we even going to get you out of the city? The governor has guards on the gates day and night."

Simon's mind swirled with ideas. "Jamal?"

Ananias shook his head. "We can't put our brother's neck on the line."

"I wouldn't allow it." Saul waved his hand, dismissing the idea.

Simon rose to his feet, pacing the room. His gaze fell to a large basket Rachel had recently finished. He lifted the woven basket and inspected it. "I think I might know a way to get you out of Damascus."

The two men stared at him.

"Remember Rahab?" He held up the basket as the foundations of a plan found footing in his mind. "But you've got to promise you'll get Salome out of captivity."

"I won't rest until she's free." Saul offered a vow.

"Then we need to get you out of town." Simon raised the large basket. "Tonight."

The moon hung low as Simon and Saul crouched in the shadows of the city walls. Silent stillness covered the streets of Damascus like a cloak of secrecy that shrouded their movements.

The familiarity of their task weighed heavily on Simon as they moved in silence. It was only three years earlier that he left Jerusalem by night, fleeing from the very man he was helping to escape Damascus. His gaze swept the darkness, searching for any sign of danger.

There was so much in that moment he wanted to say to Saul, but time was not a luxury they could afford.

Ananias appeared with Caleb and Boaz having secured the items they would need to help Saul escape the city.

Simon sent up silent pleas that his plan would work.

The night air was thick with tension. Simon led the small group moving swiftly and silently through the streets. All his training as a weapon in Barabbas' assembly proved useful as he directed the others through the streets.

When they reached the designated spot along the city wall, Simon paused. He put down the large basket and motioned for the others to prepare as he'd instructed them before they left the house.

Ananias pulled off a large length of rope from his body. "Do you think this is going to work?" his voice was barely a whisper.

"It has to." Simon helped the others to secure the ropes. His hands worked swiftly and surely in the darkness. It would not only be Saul's life he'd place in the basket, but his sister's only hope of release.

Saul stood at the ready, his eyes fixed on the ground below.

Simon checked each point before giving Saul a silent nod.

Saul stepped into the basket perched on the top of the wall and looked at Simon as he lowered himself deeper inside.

In the cloak of night, Simon saw the same fire in his friends' eyes that had convinced him of Saul's conversion. His arms ached to embrace his friend and brother once more. If it was Adonai's will, he'd see Saul again.

With another silent nod, Simon signaled the others to lower the basket.

The sounds of their labored breaths were the only noise to pierce the silence of the night.

Hand over hand, Simon helped let the ropes down over the edge. Their movements were slow and deliberate as they navigated the treacherous descent. Simon held his breath, waiting for the basket to reach the bottom.

Finally, Simon felt the rope loosen in his hands, a strong indication the basket had reached the ground below. He hurried to peer over the side.

A shadowy figure emerged from the basket and disappeared into the darkness.

Simon watched Saul make his way to freedom; a sense of satisfaction and fulfillment bathed his soul. He helped raise the empty basket and followed the others back toward Ananias' home in silence.

Settling down on his woven mat next to his heavily pregnant wife, Simon knew his bond with Saul would never be severed. Though distance would continue to separate them, their brotherhood would grow in Saul's absence. While Ananias' previous warning of the suffering awaiting Saul rang in his memory, he knew he'd done all he could to ensure his friend was safe from the dangers in Damascus.

On different courses, Simon knew Adonai had intertwined their paths, even if only temporarily. They had faced the darkness of their past together and emerged stronger and more united than ever before. Simon had found forgiveness in his enemy and grace in the sight of Adonai. No matter what lay ahead of him, Simon was ready to continue his journey of faith with courage and conviction.

Closing his eyes, he lifted a silent prayer for Saul and Salome, knowing both were secure in the hands of Adonai.

What's Next?

Bravery extends as far as the lips open.

Salome always had a hard time speaking up for herself. Being the youngest of eight siblings meant she had to fight to be heard; a battle she rarely attempted.

Without a father before her birth, her oldest brother Jesus raised her. His strong workman's arms and gentle corrective voice were the only ones she'd known.

When he revealed himself as the Messiah she longed for, Salome naturally bends to follow him. With his strength, she learns to use her voice for change.

As the Pharisees commission one of their own to hunt Way Followers, Salome speaks out against him. Her words land her in a Roman jail cell.

Can her words secure her release or will they seal her fate?

Get caught up in a tale woven with historical details and fictionalized Biblical characters that come to life in *Salome*, book 7 of the Servant Siblings series.

More from Jenifer Jennings:

Special Collections and Boxed Sets
Biblical Historical stories from the Old Testament to the New, these special boxed editions offer a great way to catch up or to fall in love with Jenifer Jennings' books for the first time.

Faith Finder Series: Books 1-3
Faith Finders Series: Books 4-6
The Rebekah Series: Books 1-3
Servant Siblings Series: Books 1-3
Servant Siblings Series: Book 4-7

* * *

The Rebekah Series:
Follow Rebekah on her faith journey through life.

The Stranger
The Journey
The Hope

* * *

Faith Finders Series:

Go deeper into the stories of these familiar faith heroines.

Midwives of Moses
Wilderness Wanderer
Crimson Cord
A Stolen Wife
At His Feet
Lasting Legacy

* * *

Servant Siblings Series:

*They were Jesus' siblings,
but they become His followers.*

James
Joseph
Assia
Jude
Lydia
Simon
Salome

* * *

<u>Paul's Patrons Series:</u>

Little known supporters of Paul's ministry have their own stories to tell.

Leading Philippi
Keeping Thessalonica
Warring Corinth
Serving Rome
Finding Colossae
Tending Crete

About the Author

Jenifer Jennings writes Historical novels that immerse readers in ancient worlds filled with Biblical characters and faith-building stories. Coming to faith in Jesus at seventeen, she spends her days falling in love with her Savior through the study of His Word. Jenifer has a Bachelor's in Women's Ministry and graduated with distinction while earning her Master's in Biblical Languages. When she's not working on her latest book, Jenifer can be found on a date with her hardworking husband or mothering their two children.

If you'd like to keep up with new releases, receive spiritual encouragement, and get your hands on a FREE book, then join Jenifer's Newsletter at:
jeniferjennings.com/gift

Printed in Great Britain
by Amazon

59414933R00126